With Beauty may you walk

With beauty before you, may you walk

With beauty behind you, may you walk

With beauty above you, may you walk

With beauty below you, may you walk

With beauty all around you, may you walk

It is finished in beauty

Hózhó náhásdlíí

—Traditional Navajo Prayer

~~Decide what you want to do, then do it~~

Claudeen Arthur,
Former Navajo Nation
Attorney General

Illustrations ≫ Kim Rouisse

Graphics ≫ Elizabeth Maxfield

SILKI, THE GIRL OF MANY SCARVES

Summer of the Ancient

JODI LEA STEWART

Bascom Hill Publishing Group
Minneapolis, MN

BASCOM HILL
PUBLISHING GROUP

Bascom Hill Publishing Group
212 3rd Avenue North, Suite 290
Minneapolis, MN 55401
612.455.2293
www.bascomhillbooks.com

ISBN-13: 978-1-935098-88-1
LCCN: 2011933008

Distributed by Itasca Books

Printed in the United States of America

For Page
For Emily
For Taylor

You are my hopes for the future, and
God holds your dreams.

Acknowledgments

Many thanks…

To the Navajo Nation for their outstanding participation in protecting this country today and yesterday as Code Talkers, Marines and soldiers; for their stance on family values; and for demonstrating a positive model of government, education, and progressive thinking to so many others.

To all the Native Americans for their bravery and service in keeping America free.

To my *Diné* friend, Sarah Ann Johnson Luther, for reading my early manuscript and offering superb suggestions regarding Navajo cultural issues. Sarah served as ambassador to the Navajo Nation as *Miss Navajo Nation* in 1966.

To Chris Eboch—author, mentor, and friend—for her gentle, effective coaching during my Institute of Children's Literature days. Her encouragement and suggestions inspired me. Her enthusiasm for my *Silki* stories propelled me into writing *Silki* novels. Her novel, *Well of Sacrifice*, showed me how.

To my husband and best friend, Mark, for his unfailing belief in my writing. Extra kudos for his knowing I can't write until the house is clean and organized, the laundry done and the paperwork up to date. Bizarre, yes…but *he* understands.

To my mother, Vivian Woods-Myrick, for her sense of humor and the fun she entwined into my psyche from early on. I am grateful for her confidence in the Silki Project. Special thanks for being the best piecrust maker in the world and for staying young no matter what. I have to admit, it's been "plenty western!" (Inside joke).

To Emily for her wonderful brand of linear humor and the sweet notes she wrote me just when I needed them. Thank you for being the sensitive, intelligent, crazy little Karate ninja that you are!

To my daughter, Elizabeth, for laughing in all the right places when reading my early manuscript.

To my son, Jason, for letting me know I had an everlasting smile.

To the other Elizabeth, long gone from this earth but not from my heart, for correcting my grammar when I was nine years old.

To Red Myrick for passing on the gauntlet of *hard work* to me. Thanks also for teaching me it only costs a nickel more to go first class. I needed to know that in my life journey.

To my late brother, Lee, for teaching me that life really is all about the laughs. I miss you so much.

Chapters

Part I

Part II

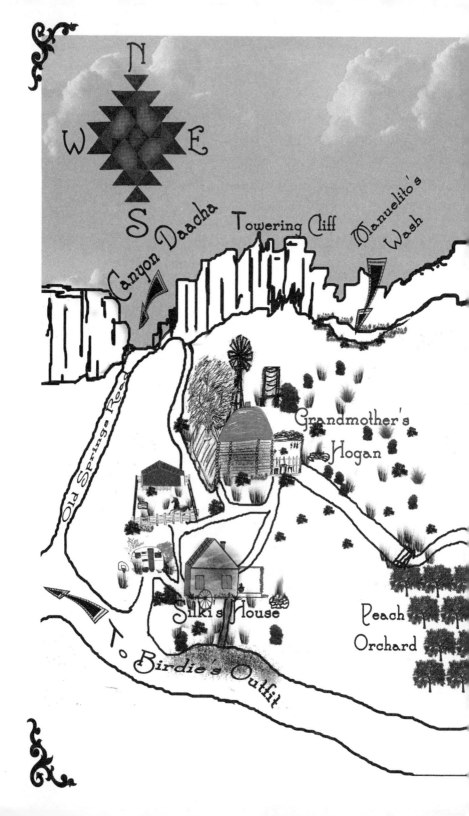

Part I

Chapter 1

Weaver Rock

BUZZY SENSATION SPREAD along the back of my neck and over my scalp like electric fingers. Until now, I'd never been scared on Concho Mountain. Guess I was just feeling weird without my best friend Birdie.

I shrugged and gave my horse, Smiles, a nudge with my heel. We headed up the mountainside to check Mustang Canyon for animal tracks and the sparkly stones Birdie and I called sugar rocks. In the blue bowl of sky above, a raven wobbled inside an air current. I started humming. Truthfully, it sounded pretty awesome.

Sneaky winds darted around the junipers and teased my hair into a mummy mask, but I didn't care. Wind was as common as red dirt here in our Navajo Nation. I inhaled a deep drink of its spicy cedar flavor and turned my face to the sun.

Just like that, Smiles planted his hooves in the rocky dirt and arched his neck so radically I nearly dropped the reins. "Whoa, boy," I said, rotating in the saddle to see if someone was behind us. Of course, no one was. Something wasn't right, though. The trees felt like they'd sprouted eyes—and they were staring straight at us. A quiver went up my back.

Smiles and I didn't budge until a woodpecker started tapping out a wooden rhythm close by. That was good. And normal. Smiles relaxed by sucking in a load of air and letting it out. The saddle and I bobbed up and down with his deep breath.

The ends of the teal and cedar green scarf tied to my upper arm snapped in soft furls. That sound usually melted me. Today it made me homesick for Birdie and the times she thought the best day ever was the one she spent with me.

Messing around Concho Mountain today was supposed to make me forget my worries, but it wasn't working. I turned Smiles around in a half circle and leaned back in the saddle. I gave him a slack rein so he could make his own way down the slope. He loved doing that. The sideways motion of the saddle leather as we descended squeaked like old times. My stomach groaned. Maybe eating lunch on top of Weaver Rock would be fun. I reined Smiles to the right.

Concho Mountain was a small mountain just a fourth of a mile from my house. It had two separate humps called Twin I and Twin II. Birdie and I had permission to explore the north side of Twin I if we didn't go near the steep cliffs marching across the top. We weren't supposed to go on the other side of Twin I, or anywhere on Twin II, until we were older—which continually made me curious. The midway marker of our lawful territory was Weaver Rock, a handsome blue-green boulder covered in lichen on one side. Only Birdie and I knew it was where the rock fairies danced when the moon was full of orange fire.

The reins slid across my palms as Smiles lowered his head to munch tender crowns of wild grass growing around Weaver Rock's base. Fresh summer smells seeped into my spirit and made me sigh. I took off the knotted scarf chain I always wore around my neck and looped it over the saddle horn. When I spread my colorful scarves along Smiles' shiny black and white neck, he turned into *Sir Smiles*, the most amazing horse on the planet.

As usual, my scarves made everything seem friendlier. Maybe it was true what my family said, that I was addicted to them. I guess they didn't mind because they kept giving me more as gifts.

I slid belly-first down the saddle fender and untied my lunch sack and Grandfather's old military canteen from the leather strings. A few steps later, a spongy feeling curled across my shoulders. It felt just like when someone gawked at the back of my head at school. I turned in a tight circle, listening. Wind shushed through the Ponderosa pines on the tall ridge beside Weaver Rock. A horned toad scuttled over part of Smiles' hoof and sat motionless near my shoe. Its spikey little head made me smile. I brushed my bangs out of my eyes and laughed aloud just to hear the sound of it.

Weaver Rock's footholds and grab places were as familiar as my own face. I made a running leap onto the side of it and stood ten feet off the ground in seconds. Breezes lifted my hair and fanned it into a cloak around my head. "I am the Queen of Concho Mountain!" I shouted, cracking up over my own silliness. This time, my laugh was real.

Kneeling, I fished a jade scarf with silver crescent moons out of my pocket and unfolded it. To keep the wind from stealing it, I weighted the edges down with the canteen and an Almond Joy. Tucked inside the scarf were relics I'd found earlier on the anthill beside Red Rocks.

Our healthy Rez ants were amazing. They found tiny pieces of history in their daily work and added them to the outsides of their pebbly mounds. Sometimes I wondered what it would be like carrying things fifty times heavier than my own weight like they did. Birdie said that was too boring, but I still wondered.

My treasures today were a yellowed bead fragment pocked with time scars and a pottery shard almost half the size of a bottle cap. I wet my finger and rubbed it over the ancient pottery piece. Two thin black lines appeared from under the dirt. Wow—a great piece for my collection.

I sipped from the canteen. Yuck. Warm canteen water tasted like metal. My stomach gurgled for food. Today, I had one of Birdie's and my favorite adventure lunches—fry bread covered with smashed pinto beans and roasted pinion nuts. I un-wrapped it from the waxed paper and missed Birdie something terrible.

Smiles snorted and jerked his head so hard his snaffle bit jingled like a dog collar in an after-swim shake. Goosebumps circled my scalp. I spun around on my rump and eagle-eyed in every direction to check for a snake or mountain lion. Nothing slithered away, and no beady eyes stared at me from the trees. I was double-dog glad of it too.

"Settle down, Smiles," I ordered in a shaky voice. His horse sense said something was wrong, but maybe he was just picking up on my morning nerves. "Hey, beauty, that rice grass tickling your hooves looks delicious."

That was supposed to be a little humorous, but Smiles neighed moodily. I waited to see if he'd start eating again. He didn't.

My Auntie Jane said it was a stupid thing not to listen to a horse. Mine was telling me it was time to leave. I jelly-rolled the relics back into the scarf and shoved them in my pocket. Shade spread over us like a tarp, and I looked up to see the sun playing in-and-out tag with a stack of clouds above Towering Cliff.

I pushed my stomach in to stop its complaining and decided I had time for a few bites before climbing down. My bread was an inch from my lips when Smiles squealed and whirled a quarter turn. I jumped so hard I kicked my candy bar off the rock. My fry bread splattered beans-side down by my foot.

As I twisted to follow Smiles' wild-eyed stare, something leaped from the rocky outcrop beside Weaver Rock to a lower ledge. An agonizing shriek filled the air—then another one—as the winged creature plunged into the trees below. It crashed noisily through the brush up the side of the mountain.

Then, nothing.

Silence surrounded us like a blanket.

Chapter 2
Trapped at the Gate

SMILES DIDN'T NEED A KICK to make him fly. A whisper of pressure from my heels and he knew what I wanted. Right now, I wanted off Concho Mountain and in Birdie's face telling her what happened.

We rounded the last foothill on the north side and cut through a corner of our family peach orchard. From there, we loped down the dirt road as if spirits were after us. Smiles' hooves pounded out a swooshy rhythm through the yellow and green rabbitbrush. He could find Birdie Yazzee's house in his sleep. My job was to hang on, and I did.

Two things pestered me on the way to Birdie's house:

1) The Ancient Ant Man. I'd been inventing crazy characters for Birdie and me to act out since kindergarten. Right before school started last year, I made up a special Watchman for the Kingdom of the Ants. Of course, He was furious at us for stealing sacred relics off the big anthill near Red Rocks. We either gave Him back our relic collections or risked severe punishment—maybe even a curse. So, was

He at Weaver Rock today? How could He come to life? I shuddered, which is a creepy feeling on the back of a galloping horse.

2) Birdie's bad habit of losing things in her bedroom. If we had to give all our stuff back, I'd have to help her. She said I was Miss Laser Memory, and maybe she was right. But we weren't actually speaking to each other right now.

Before I could stop it, my mind rudely brought up what happened between Birdie and me a few months ago.

It was one of those sharp but sweet pepperminty days in the high country when spring teases winter into moving over a little. Sunlight toasting the window glass during math period made me nuts to go adventure riding after school with Birdie. *Adventure riding* was riding our horses and pretending extreme tales at the same time.

At recess, I spied Birdie in a group of girls and waved for her to join me. She spun a beat-up volleyball between her hands as she walked toward me. Something about her seemed different. I ignored it and stretched my arms toward the bright sky, grinning.

"Concho Mountain or Canyon Daacha after school?"

"What?"

"Adventure riding, Bird. It's warm enough. Yesterday I thought up an amazing idea for us to—"

"Adventure riding?"

"Yeah. We'll stop by my house, grab some jerky and a few—"

"Gah, Silki. Aren't we too old for that junk now?"

I thought she was kidding. "Not childish stuff, silly—"

"Can't. I have practice this afternoon."

Birdie sounded mad. And she hadn't let me finish one sentence before interrupting me—very rude in our Navajo culture. She looked back at the girls by the cyclone fence. A few of them were leaning on it watching us. Birdie hugged the ball to her chest.

"Maybe you should…um, stop making up so many head stories, Silki. What if you get real and unreal mixed up, you know?"

I couldn't believe she said that. I clamped my lips shut to keep from saying what I really thought of her advice.

"I…have to go, Silki. I'll call you tonight, okay?" She walked away tossing her ugly ball into the air. I fisted away tears and watched her melt inside the circle of girls.

After that, we turned our heads when we passed each other in the hallways and sat as far apart as possible on the school bus. Oh, big surprise—she didn't call me later that day either.

Remembering had turned my face into a jalapeno. I pressed my heels deeper into Smiles' sides. He sped up. By the time we topped the last ridge, we were flying over the land. Through the uneven holes of the Yazzee's stockade cedar fence, I saw a white form in the summer brush arbor. I dipped my head and squinted, reining in Smiles from his full-throttle run. Naturally, he let me know his true feelings—he wasn't finished riding the wind yet. I had to admit he had a good excuse for acting flighty right now.

He grumbled, jerking his head up and down as he braked his hooves in the dust.

"Smiles, this is no time for back talk."

Closer, I realized the white thing was Alaska—Mrs. Anna's German shepherd. Mrs. Anna was Birdie's *Nalí* from Santa Fe. Too bad the *Queen of Volleyball* didn't tell me her paternal grandmother was visiting. That was a *first*. Birdie and I always knew everything like that about each other's families.

I scooted off Smiles keeping hopeful eyes on Mrs. Anna. I double-dog hoped she would greet me, or at least nod. Our Navajo tradition said she should acknowledge me before I went into the yard. Barging in without her invitation would be disrespectful, not to mention sorrowfully bad manners as my Auntie Jane would say. Leaving without waiting for an invitation wasn't polite either.

I fumbled with the ends of the reins. Smiles gave my shoulder a friendly push, making my bracelet clang against the hollow iron bar on the gatepost. Mrs. Anna didn't look up. She sat as straight as a doorframe on her special Two Grey Hills rug smoothed over the top of the wool blankets the Yazzees used for ground sitting when they ate outside. One time I asked Birdie why her grandmother carried that rug with her everywhere, and she said she didn't have a clue.

Mrs. Anna's bejeweled fingers twisted and pulled carded wool around the spindle in her lap. Like my grandmother, she was a master of weaving. Alaska lay across the end of her rug like an Egyptian Sphinx—head up, pink tongue dangling from a black-rimmed mouth.

I felt trapped. My insides were jumpy to get to Birdie. I started squirming.

Stop it, Silki.

Unruly behavior in front of Mrs. Anna had always felt wrong, even when Birdie and I were little. She was so different from my traditional grandmother, who had always lived just a few skips from our house. My grandmother worked outside most of her life; Mrs. Anna owned a fancy store in Santa Fe. She dressed stylishly and moved like a graceful deer. One serious glance from her eyes had the power to straighten my back like an arrow.

A pot hanging over a fire breathed mouth-watering vapors into the air. Beans! Maybe if I fainted from starvation and Weaver-Rock shock, Mrs. Anna would finally *see* me.

Judging by the sun, it was about one o'clock. At least a lacy tamarisk bush Birdie's mom planted by the gate a long time ago shaded my left arm. I curled the rein ends into a slipknot. Alaska closed his mouth and raised his eyebrows when I guided the knot over one of the gateposts. I gripped the bars of the tarnished gate with both hands like a prisoner.

What if I just crashed through the gate really fast and disappeared into the house?

Always respect your elders, Silki.

There it was—the family racket. Mother's voice. Grandmother's. My five aunts. Even Father's. How did all those voices live up there? My eyes rolled up toward my eyebrows. *Why not have a powwow while you're all talking in my head?*

Alaska's tail thumped up and down as if he had heard my head conversation. Smiles shifted his weight and sighed. Actually, he exhaled, but I knew his sounds. He wanted his tack off so the air could dry his sweaty back. I wanted to yell, *Mrs. Anna, maybe you're as cool as a frosty mug of A&W Root Beer, but Smiles and I are dissolving—*

"Your mother is teaching this summer, Silki?"

I jumped like the Arizona sky had fallen on my head, choking on my spit. "Y…yes, Mrs. Anna." Cough. "Excuse me." I cleared my throat. For a second, I worried that Mrs. Anna knew my impolite thoughts.

"What classes?" she asked.

Cough. "Uh, *Diné* Language Lab and a Natural Science."

"At the college?"

"No. College-level courses at the high school this time," I said.

Mrs. Anna's busy hands stopped. She turned her head and gazed down the road. It was hard not to stare at her. Creamy coffee skin and flowing black hair made her look more like a painting than a real person. Her arched brows and straight nose gave her the look of an empress. Even with thin white streaks swirling through her hair, it was hard to believe she was seventy-one—just one year younger than my grandmother was. Her jewelry had sparkly gems mixed with turquoise. I wondered if it was from our Rez or her store in Santa Fe.

Mrs. Anna's head snapped back to the front. Her hands dug vigorously at the spindle. "Your grandmother…still walks her worries?" she asked.

Huh? How did she know about Grandmother walking the land for hours when she was mega upset? That was inside family knowledge, and one of the few things I hadn't shared with Birdie. How could I answer Mrs. Anna's question?

The Yazzee's front screen door creaked open. A smiley face wearing glasses and topped by a fountain-spraying ponytail appeared behind the mesh.

"Silk. *Ya'at'eeh*. When did you get here?"

Birdie never looked better to me. And she was friendly! Maybe she was my *old Birdie* again. I raised my eyebrows and hoped my expression begged her to save me from our *Diné* codes of behavior. It did. Understanding danced into her eyes as she glanced from me to Mrs. Anna. She came down the steps pushing strawberry-colored frames up her nose.

"*Nalí*, you look so, um, thirsty. How about some tea?" Birdie stopped between us. She glanced at me over her shoulder and gestured with her lips for me to go into the house. Lip gesturing was our Navajo version of pointing. I sucked in a mountain's worth of relief and peeked around Birdie. Mrs. Anna nodded at me. Her eyes glistened with that strange look I'd seen so many times before. I didn't understand it any better than I understood her.

Oh well, who but elders could understand the elders?

I loosened Smiles' cinch and felt better for him as I pulled off his saddle and blanket to let air whisk across his back. I kissed his velvet nose and slipped through the gate. Passing Birdie, I whispered, "*Wol-la-chee* is alive."

Wol-la-chee was our Navajo code name for the Ancient Ant Man. We had to use plenty of code names so Birdie's little brother and all-around nuisance, Manny, couldn't figure out our business.

The shocked look on Birdie's face recharged me. Now she was part of The Weaver Rock Horror Show.

Chapter 3
Birdie's Room

I TRUDGED DOWN THE YAZZEE'S short hall with a lot on my mind. You could fry bacon on my hot scalp, and my stomach was probably searching for a new home offering more food. I jerked open the door to Birdie's room and stood there shocked to my socks. Well, actually—to my tennis shoes.

Birdie's rude behavior a few months ago had ended our get-togethers. Now her room looked more like *The Holy Valley of Volleyball* than the place I'd spent half my twelve years. A load of soggy sand dumped right into my heart. Red ants stinging my legs couldn't have hurt me as much as Birdie's room. I took a deep breath and stepped inside.

It was like being in a sports museum. Volleyball pictures and posters were everywhere. Even the cork-tiled wall Birdie's father made for our pictures and art when we were nine was contaminated. It had a magazine-sized photograph thumbtacked into the cork next to our *Best Friends Forever* sign. It was a woman down on one knee with a white ball hovering above her V-shaped arms. Black cursive writing stretched across a corner of the picture.

To Birdie. Don't let anyone steal your dreams.

Yeah, right. Didn't our dreams count anymore? College roommates and barrel-racing champions, my eye. Birdie hadn't even ridden her horse, Tito, lately. The poor thing was recovering from stitches on his front leg after tangling with a wad of baling wire in the Yazzee's corral. That was just careless—Birdie shouldn't have let that happen.

Then, a few nights ago, I almost spewed *atoo'* across the supper table when Father said Tito might spend the summer at the Tso's place. What? No one rode Smiles and Tito but us. What was wrong with that girl?

I was working myself into a fit. I kicked one of Birdie's volleyballs lying on the floor. Hard. It popped up, rolled and stalled on a pile of gym shorts and a three-ring notebook. I crashed backward onto her rumpled bed and buried my face in my scarves. Shutting out the light made me edgy after what happened at Weaver Rock. What was keeping Birdie anyway?

Uncovering my eyes, I couldn't believe what was on the ceiling—a blurry, blown-up-poster-looking thing with three smiling women in graduation gowns and caps wearing squash-blossom necklaces. Birdie's handmade paper flowers circled the poster like a halo. Underneath it were enlarged, fuzzy words telling how the women had gotten volleyball scholarships and left the Rez together to get their college degrees in New York.

Three puffy, cumulous cloud shapes floated close to the big poster. They said *New York Times, May 2003* and *Bump.Set.Spike.*

My eyes stung. My professor mother had goo-gooed *college* to Birdie and me since we were toddlers. Our plans were to be roommates at one of the eight Navajo Nation Diné Colleges. Mother was actually okay with that since some of the colleges offered four-year degrees now. She said we might have to finish our studies in Flagstaff or Tucson, but who cared? What mattered was Birdie and I—together.

It was plain Birdie's plans for college didn't include me anymore.

"Aghhh!" I yelled at the ceiling. I seriously wondered how much DelaRosa, the Yazzee's Angora goat, would enjoy eating an armful of shredded paper. I was saved from such mischief by a burning rumble in my stomach that left me feeling sick. I dug out one of the last cinnamons in Birdie's smudgy jar.

Oh-my-gosh. How old was that ridiculous candy? It was stickier than the sap Birdie and I used to scrape off trees and pop in our mouths. I picked it out with angry jerks. What next?

Birdie burst into the room like a bug-eyed bull on locoweed. I screamed my guts out. "Birdie! You scared me into another life form!"

"Me? Sheep Shears, Silki! You melted my toenails." Birdie slid down the doorframe fanning her face with her hand. She popped up instantly and rolled onto her bed. She scowled at me over her cat-eye-shaped glasses.

"Hey, what's the deal about *Wol-la-chee?*"

Bits of chewy candy scratched my throat as I swallowed. At least fear had unsealed my teeth. "Oh, just that He's actually here on the Rez. And you and I are in big trouble. But I have to go now, Birdie. I mean, what does an Ancient Ant Man have to do with…volleyball?" I said *volleyball* in my snootiest English voice. Holding my chin high, I aimed for the door, hoping with all my heart Birdie would do something—anything—to stop me.

Chapter 4
Wol-La-Chee

 IRDIE WAS FAST. Before my hand touched the knob, she materialized between the door and me. Whew. Relief.

"That's dumb. You don't come over here telling me *Wol-la-chee* is alive and just take off," she informed me, frowning like an owl in glasses.

I shook my head and groaned. "Okay, here it is. Don't go anywhere near Concho Mountain, especially Weaver Rock. That is, if you want to stay alive. You've been warned." I reached around her for the doorknob.

"Alive? What do you…?" She stopped talking and stared at my wooden expression. I slowly raised one eyebrow. I knew she hated that when we were having a fight. Making her suffer was important with volleyball stuff mocking me from every inch of her room.

Birdie throat-growled and slapped her bare foot up and down on the floor. Like a shadow passing between two trees, a sneaky plan crept into her eyes. She guided her frames up her nose with one finger. "Um, outside, I couldn't believe your messy hair. It was so…feathery. Kind of like those half-plucked chickens with the hairy skin. Yeah, that's what it was like."

I raked fingers through my bangs with both hands. "You wouldn't look so good either, Birdie Yazzee, if you'd been scared into a petroglyph and then had to stand outside a stupid gate melting in the sun," I hissed.

"A petroglyph?"

"A half-plucked, hairy chicken?"

I took a step toward Birdie. She took a step toward me. We were nose-to-nose. Mine itched. I wiggled it. Birdie's glasses slid down her bridge in slow motion. Uh-oh. That was funny. I struggled not to smile. Birdie smiled. I smiled. We resumed our serious glares, but it was useless. We cracked up. Suddenly, what Birdie said about the chicken was hilarious.

"'Scuse my feathers, but I feel kind of plucky right now," I said, one hand on my thrust-out hip and the other holding a long chunk of my hair in the air. We laughed harder, snorting crazy throat sounds.

"Birdie…" I fell onto the bed. "…remember our laugh attack that time when Mrs. West made us sit in the hallway until we got control of ourselves?"

"It took so long. You wouldn't stop acting nuts." Birdie laughed another round while I made goofy faces at her.

"Stop. Stop. My stomach hurts." Birdie dabbed at her eyes with a pajama leg rummaged from her bed. "So, why did you say that junk about *Wol-la-chee*? You crazy, chick?" She slid down the side of her bed, pulling the quilt with her. She turned and put a corner of it back on the bed, fixing it—Birdie-style.

I dropped beside her and rested my chin on my knees. I hadn't spoken to Birdie or had fun with her for so long. I wasn't ready to quit horsing around yet. Besides, making her laugh was like flying through clouds. I crossed my eyes and cleared my throat in vibrato notes scaling upward.

"Please, I beg you…no more," she said, weaving her fingers together across her stomach and smiling cheek to cheek. She sure looked like my *old Birdie* right then.

"Okay." I took a deep breath and was surprised it came out ragged. I wished with all my heart the Ancient Ant Man hadn't shown up, and Birdie and I could just go climb Red Rocks and forget all our worries.

"Well, Smiles and I went exploring this morning." I paused a few seconds before adding, "Alone."

Birdie looked down. "Mm-huh."

"You remember Nick is coming home on leave in a few days, don't you?" Birdie nodded. "Well, Mother and Grandmother have cooked up chore lists for me at least two miles long." I fell over on the floor in exaggerated tiredness.

"But didn't you go to Phoenix with your dad right after school let out?"

She remembered. "Uh-huh. He was picking up a couple of jewelry tools. We had to wait almost a week for one of them. I got to swim in the motel pool about 24/7. Oh-my-gosh, it's miserable hot in Phoenix in the summer, Birdie. I couldn't wait to get back to our cool nights. Except those dumb lists were waiting for me. Most of the stuff has nothing to do with my brother coming home."

"And…so…today…" Birdie curled her hands and pulled as if the rest of my story was a rope she had to drag out of me.

"Okay, okay. Grandmother said for me to go mess around today. Before she changed her mind, Smiles and I took off for Red Rocks like maniacs. I climbed to the top of Echo Rock at least five times. I checked out *El Anthill* too, which may be what upset *Wol-la-chee*—"

Birdie tapped her fingers on her leg. I'd almost forgotten about her lack-of-patience disease. I hoped it wasn't contagious. I continued.

"Smiles was fidgety to explore after all my climbing, so we took a run up the side of Twin I. Oh, Birdie, everything was as fresh as Grandmother's mint leaves. Breezes pranced through the tree branches like—"

"Um, Silk, I know you start your stories from the beginning of time, but can we just…" Birdie's forehead reminded me of Lake Powell on a windy day.

"Sure. Smiles-and-I-were-hungry-so-we-stopped-to-eat-at-Weaver-Rock-and-the-Ancient-Ant-Man-almost-killed-us," I said so quick my lips tingled.

"Gah, that was freaky. Wait a minute…killed?"

"Shh. Not so loud. I think we should keep this a secret. If we've done something wrong, we have to figure it out first. You know how Mother is. She might…well, just promise you'll keep it quiet, okay?"

Birdie's chest rose in a huge sigh. She looked around the room, shading her eyes with her hand. I felt a wisecrack coming.

"Hmm, no one in here. *Nali's* outside, but, duh, okay." She slid her head side to side like some of the new girls at school—they called it *the neck slide*. Definitely a *new Birdie* thing. She crisscrossed her legs and made a peace sign in the air.

Her sarcasm was mega annoying.

"You won't think you're so funny if we wind up under a curse, Birdie."

"A curse?"

"You know, *The Curse of the Ancient Ant Man*."

Birdie leaped off the floor like a centipede had crawled up her leg. Her eyes narrowed to slits. "This whole thing is one of your head stories, isn't it?"

I was on my feet and headed for the door as quick as ground lightning. Birdie's hand shot out and circled my wrist.

"Wait. I'm sorry. Just ignore that," she said.

It was hard to ignore it. How could she think I didn't know the difference between head stories and real life? I eased down on her bed lightly, ready to leave any second. Birdie sat on the floor and pushed her door shut with her foot to show how committed to my story she was now. That helped a little.

"All right, Birdie. *Wol-la-chee* is just like we imagined Him—feathered, powerful…creepy. One minute, He didn't exist. The next minute, He almost swooped us."

"Swooped?"

"Yeah. I was on top of Weaver Rock about to eat my lunch when Smiles goes all wild and crazy on me. Suddenly, the Ancient jumps off the ledge and covers up the whole sky! I think I could have reached up and touched Him with my hand—that's how close He was." I shut up so Birdie could say something. She didn't.

"Remember last August when we found those six relics on the anthill—the most we ever found at one time?"

"Mm-huh. You found that little garnet too."

"Sure did. Anyway, as soon as we had stuffed them in our pockets, the clouds thickened like boiled corn soup—don't roll your eyes, Birdie—and covered up the sun. The wind started howling. Cedar branches squeaked in pain," I said.

Birdie's eyes were statue-eye blank.

"I said a storm coming up fast like that was the Ancient's way of warning us to give everything back to the Kingdom of the Ants or—"

"He'd put a curse on us," Birdie said in a thimble-sized voice. "You were already calling him *Wol-la-chee*."

"Of course. Our Navajo name for *ant* was perfect. Anyway, guess what? Today, the sky clouded up again right before…" I paused, "…He leaped at us!"

A whole handful of Birdie's fingernails flew into her mouth. Thoughts ran around her face in circles and settled on her features like a gauzy veil. "Wait a minute. *Wol-la-chee* is bogus—a preeetend story."

She said *pretend* as if it had a slinky in the middle of it.

"You've been making these weird dudes up since we were on cradleboards, Silki."

"So what? It's not my fault one of them is real. *Wol-la-chee* jumped or flew or something over Smiles and me today. He had an enormous wingspan. And He must be huge because the brush crackled when he ran up the mountain."

Birdie stood and folded her arms in a tight knot across her chest. Her mouth was so firm her lips disappeared. I stood too, bracing for the storm.

"Silki Rose Begay, you did not see an Ancient Ant whatever. You saw a bird, maybe an eagle, but just a bird. Get a grip!"

"Get a grip? Do eagles run up mountains, Birdie? And what about his war cry, Miss Unbelief?"

"What war cry?"

"Like something in torment," I whispered.

Birdie closed her eyes and shook her head *no*. "A real ancient being? Here? Now? That's not nothing real." Birdie's grammar went out the window when she got worked up. "That's like the Lock Mess Monster or the Abonn-a-mental Snowman, or however you say that stupid word."

"Okay, what was it then? An ancient medicine man? Something else half human and half bird?"

"Well, my grandmother in Kayenta used to tell us some pretty scary stories about supernatural beings."

I paused to consider that. I didn't think any of the old traditional stories fit as well as my Ant Man theory.

The Yazzee's antique rotary telephone rang shrilly on the metal stand in the hallway. Birdie and I grabbed each other. Through the closed door, we heard the scrape of the phone receiver lift off the base. We gasped. A few seconds later, Manny delivered a monotone message with his lips smushed against the keyhole.

"Silki, your mom. She's going home from the school. She said for you to go home too."

Birdie and I let out mile-long sighs. Birdie clucked her tongue. "Little dork. He's always sneaking around spying on me."

I wanted to save our lives, not talk about Manny. "Look, I can't let *Wol-la-chee* pollute our favorite places. I'm giving all my relics back to the ants. You have to, too. He won't be satisfied with just half."

"Like I know where all mine are," Birdie said. She scooped up a white, green, and blue ball with "Mikasa" on the side and spun it on her index finger. Wow. Where did she learn to do that?

"What if we went to Weaver Rock right now?"

"Let's go," I said, accepting her challenge.

"You know I don't believe in this kind of junk, don't you?"

Did she mean I made the whole story up?

"Birdie, give me a big, fat break. I can't help it if you weren't with me today. I mean, whose fault is that? But I saw something not…not normal. Deal with it."

Birdie tossed her ball up and down in quick loops. "Let me think about this," she said, not looking at me.

I stared at the girl who had been my best friend since I'd learned to walk and talk. Honestly, she looked like a total stranger.

Chapter 5
Hozho *or Bust*

RAINDROPS HAMMERED OUT a knobby rhythm on the roof of the pickup truck cab. Silence sat between Mother and me as we rolled through our town of Mesa Redondo. When my mother wanted to talk to me, she asked me to drive somewhere with her. She hadn't been talkative while we gathered beans, milk, yogurt, red onions, fruit, and a big sack of Blue Bird flour for Grandmother at the store. I was used to it. When she was ready, she'd speak her thoughts.

Anyway, I had my own thinking to do. Birdie's reaction this afternoon was pitiful. If she were the one who had been terrified by *Wol-la-chee*, I would have dunked my head in the horse trough, screamed, and run around in circles to show her how scared I was for her. Most of all, I would have *believed* her. We weren't liars—we were best friends. Her parting words this afternoon bounced off my brain like a rubber ball.

Let me think about this—that's the best she could say to me?

I studied the muddy droplets perishing with each swipe of the windshield wipers. My life felt about safe as those drops right now. How dangerous was *Wol-la-chee* anyway? Would He go away if we gave our relics back? Was I supposed to figure all this out by myself? I shook my head in disgust. Thanks Birdie. Thanks a lot.

I glanced at the side of Mother's face. An unusual longing to share my life with her almost made me cry. I double-dog wished I could tell her how my *old Birdie* seemed to be missing, and how the *new Birdie* was squeezing my heart into a painful lump. I wanted to tell her how terrified I was at Weaver Rock today and how much I missed Nick—just like I knew she did. I pinched scarf knots and stared at her profile.

What was my mother like as a kid? Did she ever play? Of course, she'd never imagined anything—she was too serious for that. She definitely wasn't into magical stuff. If I told her about *Wol-la-chee*, she'd probably go wacky and ban Smiles and me from roaming the Rez this summer. I couldn't take that. Almost worse, she might volunteer me as a test subject for more of her professor friends' projects. I was already trapped inside one of those.

Ka-ching—the price of telling my mom was too high.

I felt lonely. Maybe I could wish for a miracle, something like: News flash! Birdie grows up!

Mother still wasn't talking. I slipped off my scarves and poked them behind me. I rolled down the truck window and peeked at Mother to see if she cared. She was lost in her own thinking world. I offered my arm to the drops outside. The shower was gentle, what our people called a *female rain*. Ozone left by the lightning and damp plant perfume filled my nostrils. The early evening light through the wet atmosphere made the sky a greenish coral. I closed my eyes. Soft pings of water splashed off my open hand.

"…it's only a few days a week. Jane and Zim need your help, you know?" Mother said.

When did Mother start talking? Why did two of my aunts need my help? Did I fall asleep? I shook my head and pressed the window button. My arm and the front of my red shirt were soaked.

"When Zim finishes her bookkeeping course, we won't get to see her and Jesse so often."

My Auntie Zim and her three-year-old son, Jesse, were moving to Albuquerque to work for my Auntie Blue Corn and her husband in their construction company. What did that have to do with me?

"So, you'll help me at the high school on Monday and Wednesday mornings. Zim just needs you and Jane to watch Jesse on Tuesday and Thursday mornings."

Me babysit?

Mother was quiet to give me time to digest her words. *Diné* did that. I was speechless anyway. I wasn't used to adult duties. Birdie and I never did anything but ride our horses and mess around all summer. Oh, and take a few trips. Usually together.

Shiny eyes turned toward me. Below them—a smile splitting the lower half of Mother's face. Uh-oh. Time to discuss her latest and greatest pet project—*Diné Bizaad Ya'at'eeh*.

"Of course, while I'm teaching my classes, you'll be in the library testing our new language program. Professor Jay and Professor Shirley are enthusiastically waiting for our notes as you progress," Mother said, her voice sounding like ten Christmas mornings all wrapped into one.

She was talking about the Navajo language CDs and DVDs she and her two friends had worked on the last couple of years. Their dream, they said, was to make our native language—*Diné Bizaad*—easy, fun, and available to everyone in the Navajo Nation.

The *Diné Bizaad Ya'at'eeh* project was supposed to be so thrilling that it made everyone foamy-mouthed to learn and learn, every minute of every day. At least, that's how they all sounded when they explained it to me a few months ago. I nodded so much—politely, of course—that my head toppled off my neck, rolled out the door, and stopped beside Smiles as he grazed behind the barn. Maybe I imagined that; but afterward, I don't remember much except moving lips and blinking eyes.

I wanted everyone to learn our language too. But why was I always volunteered as the test subject for Mother's and her friends' educational projects? Did I ask them to learn barrel racing? Rock climbing? A little wheel turned in my stomach. I was morphing into a professional test rat.

"So, pretty simple," Mother said. "You'll be a little busy four mornings a week. For a month. Of course, Silki… it's the right thing to do. Zim could use your help getting *hozho* back in her life."

Hozho was our Navajo word for harmony and balance. In everything, the *Diné* sought to live and walk in *hozho*. Mother's eyes glazed over. "What's nobler than that?"

Why should I be expected to help a grown-up with something as important as harmony? I scrunched further back into the seat. A big, bull-headed mad attack was settling in when, like a match striking on a rock, a thought flared in my mind. Maybe *Wol-la-chee* needed the same thing as Auntie Zim and the rest of us. Maybe the Ancient's *hozho* was upset because Birdie and I took that old stuff. He just wanted it back where it belonged. Then He could peacefully return to wherever Ancients go when they're not breaking through time barriers. Yeah.

Hopefully, Ancient Ant Men didn't carry grudges.

I looked at Mother's foot on the gas pedal. Wow. We were moving at the *speed of snail*. That meant she had more to say. She eased the truck to a crunchy stop on the gravel outside our house and cut the engine.

"You don't think Smiles would mind sharing you for once, do you? I think I've been pretty patient with him up to now." She locked eyes with me. Her words shocked me.

When I combined them with the look on her face, it hinted that I was probably selfish. My head felt achy.

I looked past Mother out the side window. The rain shower was over, and the sun shared its last pink glimmer through greyish blue cloud strips. I watched the bright ball ease below the edge of the world.

Mother was waiting for a reaction. I gave her one. I raised both eyebrows and crinkled out a closed-lip smile. On a scale of one to ten on my *Good Reactions Scale*, that was a measly *one*. It was all I had right then.

Climbing out of the truck, I thought about how losing harmony just wasn't the Navajo's or the Ancient's way. So, why was I losing mine?

Chapter 6
Grandmother's Eyes

I N MY HALF-ASLEEP WORLD, I remembered it was summertime. No catching the school bus. It was Saturday too. Goodie. I wiggled under my covers. From the curtains behind my eyelids, Smiles and I loped swiftly through the rain over the fragrant earth. The edge of Towering Cliff loomed ahead. I leaned forward and whispered into his ear.

"Jump, beauty."

Smiles' metal shoes clattered on the granite cliff top. His body transformed into an arrow of speed as he jumped off the rim into the great space above the Valley of Remembrance. I turned my face up to the raindrops and shouted with glee.

A loud shriek pulled our attention toward Red Rocks. A lone figure stood on top of Echo Rock, its feathers rippling in the blowing rain. It stepped off into a free fall, then broke into flight. It zigzagged above the open chasm. The sky darkened as it neared us. I gasped for air but had none. I heard words.

"The sun must find you awake to count you among the living."

I reached for more covers and felt a hand.

"Aghhh! Help! Help!" I tumbled off the bed pulling my summer blankets with me. Had *Wol-la-chee* found me in my room?

My dream fog melted and Grandmother's form angled toward me in the soft blue light before dawn. One of her hands rested on my bed, the other propped on her hip. She clicked her tongue and shook her head.

"Oh, *Shimasani*. You look so much better than a creature flying in the sky."

Her eyes widened. "Come—before the sun finds you not worth counting." She left to wait outside.

My grandmother still spun and dyed her own yarn made from sheep's wool. She created most of her natural colors with plants, roots, berries, twigs, lichen, and leaves we gathered nearby. On gathering mornings, I always set my Big Ben clock alarm to go off twenty minutes before sunup to keep Grandmother from floating into my room like a ghost. It was weird that I forgot to do that. My mother's big talk last night must have crowded out my good sense.

I pulled a bright yellow and blue striped shirt over my head and found my bib overall shorts hanging lopsided on a hanger. Halfway through a yawn and stretch, I froze.

Sheep Shears! Grandmother might be planning to gather her ingredients around Concho Mountain or Red Rocks today. With *Wol-la-chee* jumping around up there, that would be too dangerous for us. How could I loop my grandmother in the opposite direction toward Towering Cliff? She wasn't exactly easy to control.

Think, Silki, think.

Ideas raced around the track in my mind as I brushed through my tangled hair and gathered it in a figure-eight knot at the back of my head. I punched out the insides of my collapsed gathering bag and felt for my pouch of digging tools inside. I hit the kitchen for plastic bags, a few sheets of paper towels, a carton of yogurt and a spoon. I funneled five or six blueberries into the yogurt and closed the kitchen door gently so I wouldn't wake my parents. They weren't as traditional as my grandparents and my Auntie Blue Corn were—they didn't always rise before the sun. In fact, Mother got tight-lipped with me if I woke her before seven on Saturdays when she wasn't working. If my earlier yells had awakened her, she'd be up growling a little and making coffee.

It was light enough outside to see Grandmother's eyes boring into me as I walked toward her sipping yogurt from the carton. Maybe it was because everyone in my family except me hated yogurt. Or, maybe it was the bluish-pink mustache I probably had above my top lip. But those eyes were intense.

"What?" I asked.

"You look a little like my brother—Hosteen Cray—when he was young and ate the green persimmons that time. It puckered him up. He drank an Alka Seltzer in some bicarbonate of soda water to stop his belly aching. He foamed at the mouth a long time."

I nodded and looked thoughtful. I'd learned it didn't pay to say anything back to Grandmother's odd family comments like that. "I'll use my spoon," I said and patted my mouth with a paper towel.

She turned toward the track leading to Concho Mountain.

"Grandmother!" I yelled, louder than I'd intended. She turned. "Did I mention the lupine plants Smiles and I saw near Towering Cliff the other day? They're gigantic! And the desert paintbrush is flowering like crazy up there in the washes. It's much prettier than last year. Lots thicker than the ones I saw near Concho Mountain." I pointed north, grinned hugely, and held my breath to see if she'd go for it.

I wasn't lying. On the sunny side of the cliffs, I really had spotted a lot of the things Grandmother used for making tan, greenish yellow, and other color mixtures. But if her mind was set on lichen, or sagebrush to boil in her enamel pot for a bright yellow dye, or juniper twigs for a mordant, she'd ignore me.

It was no use to get in a hurry for Grandmother's answers. Underneath her stony expression ran a river of deep thinking. At least, that's what Grandfather always said.

I dropped the empty yogurt carton into my bag, waited, and looked around yawning.

Early morning was different from any other time. The air was chilly, but kind. Mr. Sun barely blinked above the rim of the world behind Red Rocks. He was already busy shooting gold specks onto tiny clouds rolling across the sky. I yawned again.

Without uttering a syllable, Grandmother walked toward me. I thought she was going to pass me by, but she stopped and fixed me with a frown and *those eyes.*

"This summer, you will learn the *Hogan Biyin,* the Song of the Hogan. While we weave."

Why did she say that right now? I stared into the dark depths of her eyes. What was in there? Resolution—pools of it. She was going to make double-dog sure I learned the old ways of our people or else.

I sighed and fell into step behind her, glancing over my shoulder at Concho Mountain. Just like that, my mood fell into the dirt. Imagine me, Silki, scared to go to the places of my heart. Who did that Ancient think he was, anyway? Did he have to be so *hozho*-challenged at the beginning of a great summer?

Grandmother's Nikes were soundless on the path. Her gathered cotton skirt swished. My purple hiking boots came down heavier with each step. I felt like clomping, so I did.

Nothing was working out right. The Navajo Nation Fair was a few months away in September, and I longed to compete in the barrel races. I would already miss next month's junior event in Window Rock because I wasn't up to performance speed.

When would I have time for Cousin TeeShirt to coach me on the barrels? Would Mother find more projects for me after *Diné Bizaad Ya'at'eeh*? Would I have any time for Nick when he came home? Why did Birdie love volleyball so much anyway?

Summer flashed through my head like a strip of movie film.

Frame one: I weave beside Grandmother.

Frame two: I walk all over *Dinéteh* gathering a zillion things for dyeing yarn.

Frame three: I chase a squirming Jesse so Auntie Zim can get her *hozho* back and I am rescued from selfishness.

Frame four: I sit in a glass box in front of a computer. I am sweating as I study the whole *Diné* language. A horde of professors gawks at me. They tap the sides with pointing sticks and put binoculars up to the glass. I am grey and hairy with a long nose and whiskers—just like a laboratory rat should be.

Last frame: I leap onto Smiles and lope to Red Rocks. *Wol-la-chee* jumps from behind a pinion pine to annihilate me or suffocate me with feathers or…

Grandmother stopped. I crashed into her back.

"Oh, I didn't see you. I…just…" The expression in her eyes turned my blathering into air.

"Listen, Silki. What do you hear?"

I listened hard. "Uh…sparrows maybe, and definitely two mourning doves."

"What do you smell?"

"Smell? Dirt…um…sage and…possibly damp sumac?" Grandmother's eyes burrowed into my heart. Sunshine warmed the back of my neck. A breeze tugged at the hair escaping my hair knot and blew it across my face like a sigh.

Grandmother's brown face smiled. So did mine. For that moment, my worries flew far away.

Chapter 7
Summer School

ROM INSIDE THE SWIRLING MIST, a voice barked, "You will talk!" A sharp light beam aimed straight into my super-glued-open eyes. I contorted in pain from the naked-eye shock. Mother's voice swam to me through the harsh brightness.

"Why don't you wear your sunglasses?" she asked, pushing her visor down and frowning at me as if I'd sprouted another head.

"These are softer," I mumbled, pulling my scarves over my eyes. The early morning sunbeams flashing through the truck windshield really had *felt* like war torture.

Driving to Mesa Redondo from our place took fifteen to twenty-five minutes on the dirt road, depending on the rut conditions. Driving on the state highway afterward was like driving on satin. We weren't far from the cattle guard that separated the dirt road from the highway when wash-off ruts grabbed the truck tires. We shook like the paint bucket I saw on the mixing machine at Lowe's in

Phoenix. My arms vibrated. My head whipped back and forth against the back of the seat.

Rain on the Rez—good for the people and the land. Bad for roads and necks.

Mother's annoyed sighs aroused me from my scarf haven. Ahead of us, Mr. Nakai crept down the road in his flatbed truck. It was fun watching calm people turn jittery as they figured out a way to pass Mr. Nakai. Right now, Mother's fingernails tapped the steering wheel, and her left knee bounced up and down.

Father said Mr. Nakai was a genuine junk man. It was normal to see him on the roads several times a day. Anything from rusty vehicle parts to a load of watermelons might be underneath the tarp covering the back end of his truck.

I giggled into my arm. His truck was hilarious. Posts plastered with chicken wire wobbled like unattached celery stalks on the flatbed. They shimmied as he dipped in and out of road grooves. The top of the army-green tarp attached to the posts creased into "X" shapes with the wheel movements. The whole rolling disaster wore a chalky caliche dust coat.

The truck bobbled to the side of the road. A skinny brown arm attached to a knotty hand waved at us to pass. Mother and I smiled our thanks to Mr. Nakai as we drove by. He smiled an almost toothless grin back at us.

≫ ≫ ≫

I made student copies for Mother and brought her coffee from the teacher's lounge. In the Language Lab, I checked computer hookups and put workbooks and handouts by each station. "Why didn't you use this class for your language project?" I asked, wishing she had.

"Because my students in this summer class have studied *Diné Bizaad* at least two years," Mother said. She leaned against the edge of the teacher's desk and folded her arms in front of her. That certain professor look came over her face. "On the other hand, our current project is graduated for learners your age, or younger, with partial knowledge of the language. Or for those who've never studied our language at all. Of course…"

I nodded politely and leaped into action rechecking computer cord plugs on the floor to save Mother from a full-blown attack of her *TMI Syndrome*. Over the years, I'd invented ways to help her through her fits of Too Much Information.

Soon after her attack, Mother shooed me off to the library with her prized discs packed in a red and black case. I stared at it. "A ladybug case, Mother?" She looked unconcerned and shrugged.

"Something one of my students gave me last semester. Thought you might get a kick out of it."

Ah, a gift. For making me suffer through her radical, month-long project. If she really wanted to make me happy, she should have rigged me up to study at Red Rocks with Smiles looking over my shoulder. The thought of Red

Rocks sent sad ripples into my soul. I just had to get those ants happy again.

The Media Center in the high school library was actually two regular-sized library tables pushed up against a wall. Dividers made two computer stations at each table. I waved at the girl behind the Resources counter. We'd sort of met earlier when I walked up just as she turned from using the copy machine. I stepped to my right, and she stepped to her left. In unison, we stepped to opposite sides.

"I'm sorry," she said, her malachite-green eyes sparkly from the light pouring in from the overhead windows. I mumbled something, but I don't remember what. I was too awed by the reddish-brown waves of hair flowing past her waist.

At the counter, I asked the longhaired girl for a computer microphone and earphones. She plundered underneath the counter while I cased the room. High school and college kids taking summer courses were everywhere. Whoosh. Did I look like a measly seventh grader or what?

The girl straightened, handing me a black box.

"Thanks. I'd bring the earphones from home, but they're from a PlayStation thing, my brother Nick's—really ancient. He's a Marine now. He's coming home on leave in a few days. Hey, you must be new here. Your necklace is so pretty." I stopped and took a deep breath.

Stop it, Silki.

My bad habit of babbling when I was nervous had struck again.

The girl studied me for a few seconds. I couldn't blame her—I didn't always act *Diné*. She placed her hand over her silver chain and held the carving at the end toward me. A delicately carved turquoise horse with a billowing mane pawed at the air with its front feet. The eyes, hooves and tips of the ears were inlaid coral.

"I've never seen a horse like this one," I said, tracing the perfectly carved lines with my fingers. "And my dad is a silversmith."

"Really? My father made it…a long time ago," the girl said.

I looked up. Did her voice quiver? I let go of the necklace. The girl sidestepped to straighten a pile of pink pads.

"Well, um, my name is Silki," I said.

"Cool name. Unusual." She extended her hand for me to shake. "Does it have anything to do with those pretty scarves you're wearing?"

"Kind of. It's a long story." I sawed her hand up and down a few times. Shaking hands wasn't a very common Navajo custom.

"Well, Silki, I'm Germaine—but call me Geri. My mother was from Ireland."

Wow. Irish and Navajo.

"I'll be a part-time senior here next semester."

"Part time?"

"A couple of my credits didn't transfer, so I'm taking two classes here and *Diné* College full time," Geri said.

"Hey, my mother teaches at that college. Usually. This summer, she's teaching a couple of classes here. I'm the official tester for her *Diné Bizaad Ya'at'eeh* Project." I rolled my eyes. "For a whole month."

"Oh." Geri bit her lip and looked down. "I'm glad we met, Silki. I just moved here from California a few weeks ago."

"Oh-my-gosh. Are you in Rez shock?"

"A little, but I lived here when I was young. The Rez seems to stay with you wherever you go." Geri busied herself moving things around on the counter.

Natives consider it rude to ask too many questions, especially on a first meeting. But I wanted to ask Geri about a thousand things. California? No wonder she wanted to shake hands. What other customs did she bring with her? And why did she get so upset when she mentioned her father?

I sensed something mysterious, but I had enough to handle getting *Wol-la-chee* happy and back into his own world.

Still, I wished I could ask Geri about the design painted on her fingernail. It was as if I'd seen it somewhere before… but where—in a dream?

Chapter 8

A Feather and a Deck of Cards

SQUINTY EYED AND CLOSE to a brain explosion—that was me sitting in front of the computer in the high school library a couple of days later. The clock over the exit doors was messed up too. No normal clock moved that slow.

I clicked into an on-line calendar and calculated. After today, two sessions down and six to go to finish Mother's project. Six? Endless. I slumped onto my elbows and pushed my eyebrows up with my index fingers. If my family gave me one more chore list, I'd turn into a cleaning rag. Worse, if Smiles and I had to stay away from Concho Mountain much longer, my heart would probably shrivel to the size of a peach seed.

My screen clicked over to an aquarium screen saver with fake fish swimming over blue gravel. I wasn't used to living inside a computer screen. I needed human contact. More than that, I needed horse contact. I stretched on my way to the Resources counter.

"*Ya'at'eeh*, Geri."

"Oh…hi." A pink line spread across Geri's cheeks.

"You look absorbed over there," she said.

"Uh-huh, but I'd rather be riding my horse." I yawned. "It's a little better than I thought it would be. *Diné Bizaad* is rough if you don't make it fun."

"Den neh beh—?"

"You know, the native language of *Diné*…us."

Geri looked at her hands. "I'm afraid I don't remember our language, Silki. I want to relearn it, though."

Embarrassing. I'd made Geri feel uncomfortable. An idea hit me. She could borrow the ladybug over the weekends. I asked her if she'd like to.

"Would your mother think it was all right…someone borrowing her special project?"

"Geri, my mother wants the entire universe to think *Diné Bizaad Ya'at'eeh*, you know? Oh, sorry. That means *the Navajo language is good.*"

Geri looked all shiny. I felt better, but I needed outside air. I pushed hard on the double exit doors and smacked into someone.

"Oh, I'm sor—" I said, but then stopped talking. Some of the morning classes had let out early. Students in groups, pairs, or alone clogged the breezeway in front of the exit doors. No one seemed injured from a door thump, so I shrugged it off. Sure did feel like a hard hit, though.

I sucked in fresh air as if I was starving and it was my food. Friendly sunbeams reminded me I'd be home with Smiles in less than an hour.

Back in the library, my sun-drenched eyes saw sunspots everywhere. I blinked hard to make the amoeba-like blobs disappear. I wobbled to my workstation. Why did the sunglasses I left on my notebook look like a turkey feather? Were my eyeballs scorched? I squeezed them shut. When I opened them, a tiger striped feather with a rounded tan and white tip lay across my notebook.

Something about that feather reminded me of wings stretching across a blue sky. I closed my eyes remembering *Wol-la-chee's* screams. My heart went into staccato-beat mode. My eyes bulged underneath my eyelids. I opened them fast before they could explode into eye Jell-O.

Knock it off, Silki.

I had to admit I had a pretty good imagination. I sat down in the chair and thought things over. Okay. If I found my sunglasses, the feather would mean zero. It had just drifted onto my notebook accidently. That was logical, right?

I brushed the feather off my notebook and looked under it. I checked inside my backpack. In my pockets. On the floor. On top of my head. No sunglasses—just that ridiculous feather burning a hole in my life. Using a

Kleenex, I picked it up and put it inside a zippered pocket in my backpack. Hard evidence like that had to make a believer out of Birdie.

I slung my backpack on my shoulder and headed for the Resources desk. "Geri, was anyone around my books while I was outside?" I asked, sliding the ladybug case toward her.

"I just came back from my break. Something wrong?"

"Sort of. Will you let me know if anyone turns in a pair of sunglasses with sunflowers painted on blue lenses?" Geri scribbled on a sticky note.

I paced the hallway outside Mother's classroom. Her natural science class was running late. At last, her students filed out. Mother followed, carrying her tote bag and wearing a satisfied smile that faded when she saw me.

"You're flushed. Have you been in the sun?"

I flashed her one of my favorite Miss Navajo Nation smiles. "No, I'm good. Definitely great," I nodded as backup to my words.

As great as any cursed person can be.

Scenery whizzed by my side window on the way home. A blizzard of questions flurried inside my mind. Questions like...what if Birdie really has lost some of her anthill treasures? She isn't exactly organized. Did *Wol-la-chee* make Himself invisible and follow me to school today? If He could show up there, no telling—

"Odd thing." Mother's voice interrupted my thought storm. "When I went back to the lab after break, my bottle of hand sanitizer was gone. Disappeared."

"What do you mean *disappeared?*"

"Just as I said. After first period, I went to the teacher's lounge for a few minutes. When I went back to the classroom for my tote bag... no sanitizer. A brand new oversized bottle too."

I couldn't swallow.

"And the most peculiar thing—a deck of Ace playing cards was propped up against the tissues. An old, soiled box of cards. It wasn't there earlier. I surely would have noticed something like that.

Cards? That was loco.

"I wrapped it in a tissue. It's in there." She pointed to the green and white striped canvas bag on the floorboard. I moved my feet as far away from it as possible.

"I probably should have tossed it, but it intrigued me." Mother clucked her tongue. "Talk about strange."

No, I didn't want to talk about *strange*. I was living *strange*. And it all pointed to *Wol-la-chee*. Now he was playing tricks on my family. Did the cards mean He would *deal* with Birdie and me? He probably left the turkey feather as a reminder of what happened at Weaver Rock—as if I could forget.

If He knew so much about me, didn't He know I intended to give everything back to the ants? I buried my face in one of my favorite older scarves—a gift from my Auntie Chooli in Oregon. My breathing sounded jagged inside the Chinle sandstone red and silver-ash stripes. I peeked out at the road ahead. Why couldn't my life just be like it was before?

Chapter 9
Birdie is No Help

SHARING MY SCARY NEWS with Birdie was a big fat dud. I called her house as soon as we got home. Manny took the message, but Birdie didn't call back. I called again. Manny said he forgot to tell her the first time. Now she was at volleyball practice and supper with her team.

I paced to the barn and back. After about my tenth trip, Smiles ignored me. I swung on the corral gate, but I was getting too big for it. It sagged into the sand. Great. Another fun thing I had to give up.

I wondered what my family would say if I exploded into dust from so much worry? Like most Natives, my kin were pretty laid back. I could imagine them saying something like, "Hmm, look at this. Silki left a pile of dust for someone else to clean up."

When I got home from Auntie Jane's house the next day, I called Birdie again. She answered. I tried not to rush or let my voice get squeaky while I filled her in about the

sunglasses, the feather, and Mother's hand sanitizer. I saved
the part about the dirty box of cards for last. My *old Birdie*
would have leaped on Tito's back and been at my house in
about fifteen minutes. We would've hopped and howled as
soon as she dismounted.

The *new Birdie* said, "Wow."

That's it—*wow*. Not even in her worried voice. She
could have been saying *whistle* or *kidney*. It definitely rated
a minus-ten on my *Good Reactions Scale*. I ignored *Her
Royal Blah-ness* and told her the plan.

"Birdie, be here in the morning with all your relics.
About eight. Father and Grandfather are refilling drip
buckets in the peach orchard, so we'll have protection if
we need it. A whole week has already passed since *Wol-la-
chee* almost attacked Smiles and me. We have to hurry."

"Well, Silki…"

"Have you even looked for anything yet?"

"Not really," Birdie said.

"Do I have to do it all myself? Sheep Shears, Birdie,
that's—"

"Okay. Okay. I'll look," Birdie said in a tone that let me
know I was a big pain.

≫ ≫ ≫

I was in Nick's trailer pulling the black and green
curtains off the windows so Grandmother could wash them
when Birdie came wobble-pedaling down the rutted trail

from the road. She was riding Paul McCartney, the bicycle she'd recently inherited from her dad.

Honestly, who but a pinion nut would give up riding an excellent Buckskin horse with a shiny black mane and tail for anything—especially a lime green 70s bike with a dull-black plastic seat. Who cared if it was Mr. Yazzee's special bike an eon ago? It wasn't Tito.

I jumped over the metal stoop underneath the trailer door to greet Birdie. No matter what, I always got happier when we were together. She balanced a worn-out Roi-Tan cigar box on one hand like a waiter's tray. I figured it was her Grandpa Pete's since he used to smoke cigars.

Birdie's front tire scraped a rock, and she struggled with her one-handed steering not to topple over. "Here's all I could find," she said, shoving the box toward me and planting her feet on each side of the bike. I checked inside.

"You're missing at least eight or ten pieces."

"I know." She yawned. "I can't remember where I hid them. Places I thought Manny couldn't plunder, I'm sure."

"I can help you find the rest after I finish—"

"Not today." She looked around with another wide-mouthed yawn. Birdie acted as if a feathered immortal threatening our lives was as normal as recess.

"Well, let's just hope this satisfies Mr. Ant Man." I felt tired all of a sudden. I took the cleaning towel off my arm and let my shoulders sag with weariness. "I may never get finished around here," I said.

Birdie ignored my shot for sympathy. She drew a line in the sand with her shoe. Could she be any weirder these days? Maybe she couldn't help it. I put my arm across her back. "Hey, come in the house and have a root beer with me. I'll show you that creepy feather. Can you imagine when I found it on my notebook, girl? I guess *Wol-la-chee* stole my sunglasses just to be mean, right? Birdie, you wouldn't—"

"Can't right now." Birdie's stiff shoulder under my arm sent ice cubes rolling into my stomach. "I have to wash my gym stuff. I have a load of other junk to do too. Mom made a list for me to get done before I go."

"Go?"

"Volleyball camp in Gallup. The bus takes off from Deer Wash Middle School at eight Monday. I just have a few days to get ready." Birdie studied the ground. A strand of hair escaped from behind her ear and draped over her cat-eye frames. She brushed it back.

"You never said anything about going to camp this summer."

"Well…" Birdie raised her head, finally looking me straight in the eyes. Her expression had changed from bored to bright. "…I didn't know I got to go. It's kind of expensive. My *Nalí* wanted to send me."

Now Birdie's eyes twinkled like glitter glue. I'd seen them like that for important things like riding the Ferris wheel or clothes shopping in Albuquerque. But for volleyball camp?

Birdie cleared her throat and offered me a puny smile.

"Look, Silki, I'll be back before the Fourth of July celebrations. We can go to the parade and hang out at the carnival. Just like always. I'll look at your feather then too. And, uh, I'll try to find the other relics for you and everything when I get back, okay?"

My feather? Find the relics *for me*? She was treating me like a baby. Or a loser.

"I'll call you when I get back. See ya, Silk." Birdie turned the bike around, pedaled a few turns and stopped. She looked back at me a few moments before pushing off.

And just like that, she was gone. I was left to handle the whole Ancient world by myself.

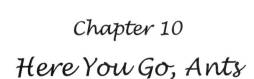

Chapter 10
Here You Go, Ants

GRANDFATHER'S KNOTS ALWAYS came in handy. He'd been teaching me how to make them since I'd learned to tie shoelaces. I patted the soft suede bag hanging from my front belt loop. Its corded strings were tied in a Figure Eight Bend knot—a bulky knot, but easy to undo. It represented how important the treasures inside were.

Last night, I'd dumped every bead, miniature arrowhead, pottery shard, chipped flint, and obsidian fragment I had into the pouch. The only thing left out was the garnet. I reasoned that the ants mined it from inside the earth, so it wasn't a relic. Shouldn't gems sort of belong to the human who found them? I thought so.

A few more neck-cracking dips and we'd be at the peach orchard. I was sardine-packed between my dad and grandfather in the narrow seat of Father's old pickup. It felt safe. Under the bill of a red and black Arizona

Diamondbacks cap, Grandfather's eyes narrowed from the glare pouring through the windows.

I wondered, would *Wol-la-chee* notice the missing pieces? That brought Birdie's image to my mind. I blew it away like dandelion fluff before it could latch onto me.

The truck wheels sank into what felt like a small canyon. "This road sure has a personality," Father said, maneuvering the steering wheel like a racecar driver. Grandfather grunted.

Behind us, strapped barrels gnawed against each other. Water sloshed over the lids. Springs groaning, Father gunned the engine until we were on level ground. Drops spraying across the rear cab window sounded like gusts of late summer rain.

When we stopped, the three of us tumbled out like marbles rolling out of a tobacco can. I watched the men unlatch the tailgate before turning to face neat rows of peach trees. Behind them, rusty boulders pushed into a turquoise sky. Veins of sandstone twinkled along their outside layers. Crows drifted lazily above Echo Rock in an imperfect circle, their feathers flashing purplish-black in the sunlight. I breathed in the sweet high-country aroma. I loved Red Rocks with a passion.

Wood thunking against metal as Father and Grandfather ramped the water barrels out of the truck broke the magic. I knew I was stalling. I took a deep breath and put one foot in front of the other.

Be brave, Silki. You are Diné.

Yeah, sure. I'd never felt less brave. Darn Birdie. Wasn't this mission as important as washing smelly gym clothes? The way I saw it, she was cruising for trouble in the seventh grade with a volleyball in her skull instead of a brain.

I made myself think light thoughts as I followed the path around the edge of Red Rocks. It seemed amazing that everything looked about the same as it did before my life changed a week ago. Even the anthill. It was still a sprawling, one-foot-high mound of red and tan gravel. The rectangular chalk rock with yellow sun winks Birdie and I had muscled over beside it last year was still in place. Whenever we stood on it, the busy red ants didn't seem to mind us watching them. Guess they'd minded a lot about us helping ourselves to their treasures, though.

Quick side-glances at Concho Mountain's two humps didn't seem too scary. I stepped up on the chalky rock and unknotted the thick cords of my pouch. I forced the puckered ruffles apart and tried to keep a sharp eye out for danger. That wasn't easy because ornery winds kept churning my hair into a tornado swirl.

The relics spilling onto the anthill caused a commotion. It probably sounded like an avalanche to the ants. Remembering all my adventures with Birdie as the pieces tumbled out of the sack made my lungs feel swollen, but I wouldn't let myself cry.

I cleared my throat to give the speech I'd practiced last night. I'd decided the wind was a good way to get the message to the Ancient since I wasn't sure if speaking directly to Him would be disrespectful. I mean, who knew his rank or anything?

"Wind, you are always here, and I think we are friends. Will you ask Mr. *Wol-la-chee* to be in *hozho* again? I, uh, I mean, Birdie and I didn't mean to disturb His Kingdom of the Ants. I hope He'll accept these old things back from us. We thought they were okay to keep since they were tiny and mostly broken. I guess we were wrong. We'll be very grateful if He just goes back where He came from now. Wind, thanks for delivering this message."

I moved from the anthill as royal as a queen of Concho Mountain should be. My mission accomplished, I was now an ambassador of Nature's Good Will. I felt pretty great. A few steps into my victory walk, I caught a glimpse of dark feathers passing behind the trees. A bird? Too big to be a bird. *Wol-la-chee?* Goosebumps traveled at the speed of light down my back and legs.

The wind picked up. Uh-oh. I didn't like that.

The two junipers Birdie and I named Two Best Friends because they grew toward each other huddled and whispered secrets. Overhead, clouds chased by wind made light and dark shadows flicker around me. By my feet, a blue and white feather with grey speckles reminded me I still had a strange feather in my backpack. I wasn't happy about the way a clump of sagebrush wiggled by the path back to the orchard.

My proud steps turned into strides. A jog. A sprint. Fear pumped right along with my blood through every vein in my body.

I ran for my life.

I tripped. Below me, I saw mean, miniature spears frowning up at me from a bed of prickly pear cactus. I leaned and hopped, missing the sharp needles by a hair. I broke into a sweat thinking of those tiny swords impaling my skin.

I landed flatfooted on a slanted rock and rocked forward onto my toes. My head led the way as I belly-flopped into the orange dirt. My face was inches from a pair of crusty boots. I looked up, gasping for air.

Grandfather rubbed his chin. "Hmm. Good run, Silki. Diamondbacks tryouts next spring." He dipped his shiny silver lard can back into the water barrel.

I wondered—would I live until next spring?

Chapter 11
An Old Photograph

HEN MY AUNTIE JANE smiled, you thought about Fourth of July sparklers. Her short coppery brown hair rose and fell in natural, roller-coaster waves. My mother's second-to-oldest sister had an easy laugh that started in her eyes.

Today, she wore a white and blue plaid shirt tucked into denim capri pants with tall navy wedge shoes. She put her fork down and ignited in a toothy smile.

"Boy howdy, Silki was a big help with Jesse this first week. He's a storm, isn't he, babe?" she asked, glittering in my direction.

I nodded, grinning back at her. I couldn't help my reactions to Auntie Jane. If she smiled, I smiled. If she laughed, I started laughing—even before I knew what was funny. Everyone said we looked a lot alike. That was okay with me because we were both horse crazy. Oh, and because she was pretty too.

"Pass the tortillas please, Jeanette," she said, and my mother passed the basket to her. "Thank you. Little Jess wanted Silki to be his practice bucking sheep for the Junior Wooly Rides this September. He wore her down, and she did it."

A ripple of grunts and chuckles spread around the rectangular pine table under Grandmother's summer arbor. I didn't think it was very funny.

Jesse was a little terrorist in overalls. The second time I helped Auntie Jane babysit him, I daydreamed of turning him out to summer pasture tied to a giant sheep. One more grab at my scarves, or tug on the ends of my hair, and I was seriously calling Cousin TeeShirt to bring us that sheep. I wondered how I'd get through the next three weeks with a three-year-old disaster.

But right before Father came to get me that day, Jesse crawled into my lap and kissed my arm. "Love you, Cousin Silly," he said, and toppled over asleep. Watching his face, I decided to hold off on that sheep request for a few more days.

What was I doing sitting around with grown-ups when I could be with my horse? "Okay if I use a little water for Smiles, Dad?" I asked. He nodded, giving me a be-careful look about the water. I rolled a couple of blue tortillas. Smiles loved them as much as apples.

I untied the long, sheer tangerine scarf threaded through the loops of my cutoffs and pulled it free while I walked down the road to the barn. I tied it in a Windsor knot and slipped it on the gatepost farthest away from where I'd be spraying water. Smiles' expectant eyes looked through the metal slats of the back corral gate. I swung the gate open. He high-stepped through, nuzzling my hand for his treat.

"I'm all yours, beauty. No school. No Jesse. No gathering plants and roots." He bobbed his head up and down. Could anyone have a truer friend? I knew I couldn't. Smiles would never forget about me like Birdie had lately.

I lost no time, or water, spraying him from neck to hoof. No one wasted water on the Rez—it was too hard to replace. The afternoon was still. Maybe the wind was busy delivering my message. Humidity steamed off Smiles' back in little puffs. I sprayed the mud off my flip-flops and led him to a high spot to use the sweat stripper on his soaked coat. I looked up from my work and saw Birdie and Paul McCartney rolling down the road from the direction of Grandmother's hogan.

"Hey," Birdie mumbled, walking her bike to a stop. "Got some more relics for you." She pulled a dime-sized, black pottery shard with white paint, three arrowhead shavings, and a semi-circle of bead out of her pocket. She poked them through the board openings. I examined them before stuffing them into my pocket.

All right. We were getting closer to finding everything now.

Birdie rocked the bike back and forth a few inches. She looked everywhere but at me.

"I guess you don't have time to go to the anthill with me, do you? You remember I took our other relics back Friday, right?" I said.

"No," was all she said.

No, *what*? No, she didn't have time; or no, she didn't remember I took the other stuff back? Birdie rubbed her hands along the rubber grips on her handlebars. I felt awkward around her—another *first*. All of a sudden, she dipped her hand into the basket bolted to the front of Paul McCartney.

"Do you know this guy?" she asked, holding up a beat-up square photograph. I squiggled under the corral and took it from her. The coating was cracked and shiny. I touched it. Sticky. The yellowed border had saw-toothed edges. A rainbow of yellow, grey, and beige stains splashed across the image in the center. Spots covered part of the face. I smelled them. Tree sap?

A Native American man in a military coat with a pleasantly serious smile gazed at me from the photograph. He had what Auntie Jane would have called a mischievous face. "Who is it?" I asked.

"Duh! I wouldn't ask you if I knew, Silki," Birdie said.

I wondered if the *new Birdie* knew how mean she sounded most of the time.

"I found it on the porch swing this morning," she said.

"It belongs to your mother...or Mrs. Anna," I offered.

"*Nalí* isn't even here, Silki."

Well, gosh. I'd forgotten I wasn't important enough to know who came or went at the Yazzee house these days. "Maybe your dad put it there." No again. "Probably blew in. The wind blows in tons of unusual things. One time I found a scorched piece of—"

"It didn't blow in," Birdie said, as if I were Dumbo the elephant. "It was stuck in the slats. Propped up. And don't say Manny put it there because I already asked him. I left my Mikasa ball on the porch swing last night. This morning, it was gone and this stupid picture was there."

"I thought you kept your volleyballs in your room."

"I do usually. We cooked out last night. I was on the steps spinning my ball and listening to Dad's stories about the old days. It got late, so Mom told me to shake out the blankets and put them in the gunnysacks. I rolled my ball over on the swing and forgot about it. I thought you might know…"

Birdie's voice faded as I stepped inside my head to think things over. Now *Wol-la-chee* was vandalizing the Yazzees. And after everything I did to help Him get His *hozho* back.

"…so now, I have to take my dirty ball to Gallup tomorrow."

"Birdie, you know *Wol-la-chee* did this, don't you?"

"No, I don't," she said, making a big deal of turning her bike around. "Gotta go."

"Your picture," I called to her back. She turned. I fanned the picture in the air.

"Trash it."

And just like that, the sad look on Birdie's face made me sad too. I was even sorry her ball was missing.

"Hey, Bird, stop by in the morning before you catch your bus. Mother and I don't leave for the high school until 7:30. You guys can drive by before that, can't you?"

"Maybe. Bye."

I stashed the picture in my pocket and walked back to Smiles shaking my head. He had been super patient, but I knew he was curious. I angled the wire brush from his crest, down his back and over each rump. I combed the tangles out of his mane and braided his forelock to make it crimped for tomorrow. Plaiting strands of his tail to mix in with the straight hair, I noticed he needed horseshoe work.

The whole time I groomed him, Smiles and I pitched all the facts around in low voices. We agreed the five new pieces were the best part about Birdie's visit today. Every relic had to be accounted for, or else. Or else what?

Smiles and I didn't have a clue.

Chapter 12
A Misunderstanding

THE KITCHEN CLOCK said I barely had enough time to finish breakfast and give Smiles a block of hay before Birdie and her mom drove by. I was running late because I had to switch out my teal and cedar green scarf for a clean one in the drawer. In a few days, I'd tie together a whole new scarf chain and hand my dirty scarves over to Auntie Jane. Grandmother said Auntie Jane spoiled me. I guessed that was true.

I shot out of the house with my eyes peeled for a strip of tangerine at the corral. The almost cloudless sky and daub of morning cool sidetracked me a little. A light wind blew north toward Towering Cliff and grabbed the ends of my hair. I examined a piece that brushed across my lips. It was dark with a few coppery glints like Auntie Jane's.

At the barn, I stared at the empty post where I'd left my scarf while I groomed Smiles yesterday. How could I forget it? Another *first*. Where was it? I guessed someone took it inside for me.

I unbraided Smiles' forelock and arranged it artfully to the side of his face. He stared me down until I gave him a few promises for later. I turned and froze like a Popsicle. A crescent moon shape of white, blue, and green peeked out from the side of the galvanized water trough. I rounded the curve of the trough and saw Birdie's missing volleyball on the ground. It just sat there stupidly, not knowing what it was doing to my insides. How could it be there? I picked it up and stared at it like it could talk to me.

The Yazzee's car horn blast almost sent me face down in the muck. Through the spaces between the corral boards, I saw the Yazzee's car driving by at a turtle's pace. Both front windows were down, and Birdie sat in the window frame on the passenger side. Her cheerful wave over the top of the car made her high ponytail jiggle. Her dark green shirt had a shiny gold number twelve on the front. The corners of her mouth pointed toward the sky. As usual, her glasses hugged the end of her nose.

Mrs. Yazzee, Aunt Susan as I called her, smiled out the driver's window with a Grand Canyon smile. She tapped the car horn in rhythm. Beep—beep beep beep—beep.

Wow, festive. I scrambled to the top of the corral. This was fun with a capital F, and I wanted in on it. "*Yá'át'ééh!*" I shouted, moving my hands in the air like a Hula dancer.

"Woo woo, Silki! See you in a…" Birdie's face sagged. She ducked her head inside the car. Aunt Susan hit the brakes hard. Their car rocked back, then forward. Little dust clouds floated up and powdered the tires.

Birdie melted into the car and out the door like a slithery snake. She tromped toward me. I could almost see lightning bolts sizzling from her eyes. It was fascinating and scary too. My maddening drawing habit made me quickly sketch her in my mind. I shrank back as she drew near.

"Birdie?"

"Why?" she snarled, her eyes thinning into hyphens. She stopped and looked down at her best volleyball caught on a clump of dry weeds. I remembered throwing it down before I climbed the boards a minute earlier. Now it jeered at me from the other side of the corral.

"I know you hate me because I love volleyball now, but stealing my ball? Trying to make me believe in your stupid Ant Man? Nothing you say anymore is real!"

My hand shot up. "Listen, Birdie. That's not true. I found your ball just a minute ago by the water—"

"You're still going to lie about it?" Birdie shook her head in disgust. "That's low."

"Birdie Shay Yazzee! Stop it right now. I didn't steal your ball. I wouldn't do that. If you don't know me better than that…" A lump in my throat choked out the rest of my sentence.

Birdie's eyes glowed with an extraterrestrial shine. "You know what? I can't wait to get away from you. Volleyball camp will be cooler than anything we ever did together. All you do any more is kiddy stuff. Why don't you take Barbie on your adventure rides?"

Her poison-dart words paralyzed my heart.

Birdie scooped up her ball and let it roll down her forearm. She kept hateful eyes on me while she spun it on her finger. Then, she stomped back to the car.

In a few moments, Aunt Susan mailed me a worried look through the open window. It said she didn't know what was going on, but she still cared about me.

Through wet eyes, their car looked like a blurry rock rolling down the road.

Chapter 13
I-40 to Holbrook

A LOCUST WIRED to a roasting stick had to be in a better mood than I was today. Interstate-40 to Holbrook wasn't my favorite stretch of road either. The bleak scenery reminded me of Birdie's back as she stormed away from me two days ago.

And where was my tangerine scarf? No one in my family knew. Of course not...that would be too easy. Nothing about this summer was easy. Take last night. I felt doom as soon as the phone rang, and I was right. Nick's thirty-day leave had been butchered down to a few days because of some dumb technicality. He promised us he'd get an extended leave in August or September, but that didn't make it okay.

I stared through the side window at the cracked earth and yellow weeds along the highway. *Wol-la-chee* had finished ruining my friendship with my best friend. It was plain He was a psycho troublemaker. I visualized him cackling crazily—my tangerine scarf tied around His head—as He rolled Birdie's stolen ball into our corral.

Now that was a strange head picture, even for me.

"Be careful when you get out of the truck," Grandfather said, tapping me on the shoulder. I looked at him, blinking to clear my mind. Wires dangled from both his ears. The CD player Mother bought him a few Christmases ago balanced on his long, bony legs. He loved music and thinking he was keeping up with the young folks. He was probably on the verge of asking for a smart phone and an Mp3 player next. He'd get it too.

Grandfather was dressed up for Nick's homecoming. An etched silver and abalone bolo tie pressed against the top snaps of his starched white western shirt. Ironed creases on the legs of his Wrangler jeans drew a straight line to his boot tops. Grandfather ironed everything, even his work clothes. It was an old habit, he said, from his Marine days. Grandmother ironed for him sometimes as a surprise. That sort of made up for her calling Marines *soldiers* instead of *Marines* most of the time, which made Grandfather grind his teeth.

Two CD cases sat between us in the backseat. Grandfather's creamy white straw Resistol hat, top side down, rested on the truck floor. My easy-going grandfather could morph into a black bear when it came to his hats. I considered that and moved my feet closer to the truck door. Grandfather was still eyeing me.

"Uh, I didn't really get what you said, Grandfather."

He pulled the earphone jack out of the player. The flute notes of Navajo Elder Kee Chee Jake escaped into the air. Grandfather's eyes sparkled playfully. "Dangerous business—your chin so low. Might trip on it when you get out."

It took a few seconds to realize he was teasing me about my bad mood. I gave him a fake fist hit to the shoulder. Grandfather enjoyed his own jokes. A lot. He laughed silently, his shoulders shaking up and down.

He switched to a Plateros CD and re-inserted the jack. He watched out the side window with his head bobbing to each side. He was happy. I should be too. Nick was safe and would be home today. In fact, I'd see him in less than an hour. I let that soak in.

Mother's new Dodge truck hugged the road like a happy cat purring contentedly down the highway. By the time we reached the Petrified Forest National Park, I'd made up my mind to tell Nick everything. About Birdie and how she was a horrible girl now. How she didn't love Tito or me or anything but volleyball. How unreasonable Mother was these days about her test projects, and, most of all, how *Wol-la-chee*'s bizarre pranks were ruining my life.

While I was thinking about rolling all that mess onto Nick's shoulders, a quivery sigh rose from the bottom of my being. It brought liberty—like I'd breathed in something good and breathed out something bad.

And just like that, I felt like singing. I tapped Grandfather on the shoulder and motioned for him to unplug. I started singing with the CD. My parents looked back at me from the front seat, then at each other.

Grandfather, Levi Platero, and I rocked us into the Holbrook Greyhound bus station at exactly 2:00 p.m.

Part II

Chapter 14

Nick

T HE SEVENTH PAIR OF FEET off the bus belonged to my brother. At the top of them—Nick. Gripping an olive green duffle bag, he stepped aside for other passengers to pass. He spoke to a man who came down the bus steps. They both laughed, and the man touched his forehead in a salute as he walked away. Nick's teeth gleamed like Auntie Jane's.

My stomach fluttered like a butterfly cage. Was my brother really here and not a zillion miles away in foreign countries? I couldn't soak him in fast enough. It was hard to believe the man standing there was actually my Nick. I read U.S.M.C. on the shoulder of his flag-blue knit shirt. It was tucked into jeans stiff enough to walk alone. Like Grandfather's. His black western boots were mirrors. He reminded me of Popeye with his bulgy arms. A military buzz still replaced his shiny dark hair.

My feet danced in a nervous pattern. I pinched scarf knots and turned begging eyes on Mother. She nodded. I flew to my big brother and squeezed him so hard my arms hurt. Just like that, I started crying. Nick pushed me away at arm's length. His eyes twinkled like winter-sky stars.

"What's this?" He lowered his voice to sound like Old Professor BeSpeckles, a character we made up one time to torment Mother on a trip to New Mexico. "Uh…tell me, college student, have you, uh, seen my little sister?" He shielded his eyes with a hand, pretending to look for me right and left. "Can you help an old man find Little Dove?" he croaked.

No one in the world called me Little Dove except Nick. I was laughing and crying at the same time. Quietly, though. We weren't a noisy family in public. "You're a loco in motion," was all I could get out. I struggled to turn off the hoses in my eyes.

"And you're the Princess of the Rez. Whew. Look at you! Father better get his big clubs ready," he said. He yanked on my scarf chain, and we touched thumbs in the air.

I swelled like a wet sponge under his brotherly admiration. If anyone could straighten *Wol-la-chee* out, it would be Nick.

Mother crowded in and wrapped her arms around Nick's neck. Father patted the top of his hair bristles and squeezed his biceps. They grinned at each other. Grandfather rocked back and forth on his heels and jingled change in his pockets. On his face—a rare Extreme Smile.

The 100-plus miles back home seemed more like ten miles. My worries about Birdie and *Wol-la-chee* were far away. A couple of times, Nick grabbed his camera from the duffle bag and caused an in-the-cab lightning storm.

"Traded a few sketches for it," he beamed at us, pointing at his fancy new camera.

He jumped from the truck before it stopped rolling.

"Little Navajo Grandmother, where are you?" he called through cupped hands. His boldness with Grandmother was unusual for our culture, but it wasn't surprising. Nick had a way with her. Yeah. With about everyone.

He ran down the path to the hogan. When the rest of us got there, Nick's face was over a pot on the stove. The lid was in his hand. Grandmother faced the wall wiping her eyes. When Nick first joined the Marines, Grandmother *walked her worries* every day. Her eyes were blistery swollen when she came home. Once, her eyelids were so puffy, I thought she'd blundered into a nest of wasps. When I asked her about it, she glared at me through bloodshot eyes for a long time. I'd never seen her actually cry, though.

We waited. Nick sneaked a fork into the pot and stole a hunk of potato. It disappeared into his mouth. He danced in front of the stove, pointing at the pot and rubbing his stomach. I giggled soundlessly. Nick was a one-man show.

Grandmother sniffed and cleared her throat. "We will eat now," she announced. All of us jumped into action, grabbing pans and hoisting foil-covered bowls lined up on the counter into our arms. We were setting the table in our kitchen when the telephone rang. Mother answered it in the living room.

"Silki, Susan Yazzee," she called.

Birdie's mom? It seemed weird to hear from her with Birdie out of town. I took the phone from Mother.

"Hello?"

"Silki, hey, I know Nick just got here. We're all so proud of him. How is he anyway?"

"The best," I gushed, bordering on delirium because he was actually in the next room.

"Good!" Aunt Susan said with high excitement in her voice. She knew how to join into fun times. "That's real good. I won't keep you. I just called to see if you and Birdie did something with our outside blankets."

"Blankets? No. I haven't seen them since, uh…oh yeah, Mrs. Anna was using them a few weeks back. I haven't been at your place since then."

"I know." Aunt Susan sighed. "Well, just thought I'd ask. Figured maybe you and Birdie cooked up something fun to do with them."

"They're gone?

"We sure can't find them. My brother Shilah and his family are coming for the Fourth. You met them, remember? They live in Two Mesas and have the three kids? Anyway, I sent Manny to air the blankets out on the fence. He said the sacks were there, sure, all folded up and everything. Just no blankets. Said he found a hunk of turquoise on top of the sacks. A rough, uncut piece. I just don't know."

"Turquoise?"

"Yeah. Did you leave it here? Maybe something out of your Father's jewelry stuff—about the size of my thumb?"

"No. Not ours," I said.

"Just a coincidence, I guess," Aunt Susan said. "Well, you get back to enjoying Nick. Tell him we want to see him before he leaves. We heard about his visit getting cut. That's too bad."

Oh-my-gosh. News spread faster than electricity on the Rez.

"Sorry I bothered your welcome-home-Nick night," Aunt Susan said.

"That's okay. Bye." I started to press the off button.

"Silki?"

"Yes?"

"When Birdie gets back from camp, you come over and eat supper, all right?"

Just thinking of Birdie made me feel bruised. I knew Aunt Susan meant *come over and get things worked out.* That wasn't okay with me right now. I couldn't think of anything to say.

"Silki?"

"Oh, uh, sure."

"Good. *Hagoonee.*"

"*Hagoonee.*"

I clicked the phone off in a stupor. The happy chatter from the kitchen sounded miles away. Pretty plain. *Wol-la-chee* was as mad at Birdie as He was at me. First, He stole her favorite volleyball. Now, it was her family's outside blankets.

Walking back to the kitchen, I felt like a zombie. Maybe I was one. Just add drool and limp arms.

Chapter 15

Scary Run

OULD I EVER LEARN the kind of patience the elders had? By the time Auntie Jane's restored 1959 GMC pickup bucked over the rough roads and landed in the gravel outside our house, I was bordering on uncivilized behavior. I wanted Nick all to myself, especially away from the phone. Ours rang every few minutes last night.

How long will Nick be here? Will he be in the parade Thursday? On horseback? In a car? Is he dancing in the Fourth of July festivities? Are we having a special party before he leaves?

In between the calls, Nick acted out stories about his Marine buddies and commanders until we roared with laughter. Grandfather was right—Nick was darn good medicine.

When Auntie Jane cut the engine, I soared out the door and into the house. No one home. I slammed down the path to Grandmother's and burst through the door.

"Grandmother, where's Nick?" Even to me, my voice sounded like a buzz saw grinding down the walls of her and Grandfather's quiet dwelling. Grandmother sat in front of her loom, humming. Humming? She hadn't hummed since Nick left for San Diego, California, almost two years ago.

Grandmother ignored me. Not a surprise. I ordered myself to calm down if I wanted to learn anything. Like most adults, especially the elders, Grandmother didn't appreciate wild *klizzies* like me crashing through her door and chewing up her harmony. I switched to slow-mo and squatted beside her.

"Your rug is growing more beautiful every day, *Shimasani*. Can you believe I'll be finished helping Mother, Auntie Jane, and Auntie Zim in just two more weeks?" I said, mimicking Barbie's cheerful voice on my old *Rapunzel* DVD.

I hoped Grandmother was picking up on my enthusiasm for her projects. Her high-pitched humming mixed with the ticking of the antique wall clock Father gave her when he married Mother were driving me up the wall. My foot wanted to jiggle. Grandmother lifted the heddle stick on the loom and shoved a batten through the warp to hold it open. She took her time inserting a strand of silver-green yarn I'd seen her dye with boiled sagebrush twigs and leaves. I wanted to howl, *why is everything moving so slow?* But, of course, I didn't.

Something smelled wonderful. I sneaked a look at the stove. A stainless steel pot with melted black side handles sent savory steam toward the high log ceiling. Yum—Grandmother's dried corn soup. My belly went into its usual *I'm-so-starving-must-eat-now* mode—just about making me lose focus on finding Nick. I threaded my fingers together and pressed them against my stomach to stop its complaining and started back in on Grandmother.

"Gathering will be so great this Saturday morning," I said, flashing both rows of teeth at the side of her face. I waited. "We'll probably start learning that hogan song next week, right? I can't wait."

Grandmother's lips curved into a smile. "It is good that Nick walks our sacred land," she said, combing the thread into the rug.

Oh, whine. Our *sacred land* was about 27,000 square miles and larger than the state of West Virginia. I willed myself to ask my next question as if I had a comma after each word.

"Which, part, of, our, sacred, land, *Shimasani?*"

"High up toward the morning," she answered, in her own good time.

Got it. Nick loved climbing Red Rocks as much as I did. They were high, and sat to the east of our outfit where the sun rose each day. Grandmother made me work for the answer to pay me back for being in such a hurry.

I yawned noisily to show Grandmother how peaceful I was. "Thank you, my grandmother. I'll be back later to help you cook the meats." Tomorrow marked the day our family would jump into the Fourth of July activities in

Mesa Redondo. We'd fix food tonight, and more after the parade tomorrow morning.

Inch by inch, I lifted off the floor. Behind Grandmother, I took stretchy steps toward the door and collided with Auntie Jane and her mammoth straw purse in the doorway. She smelled like flowers. Red-bib lettuce and green onions from Grandfather's garden sprouted from her hands. She smiled. Naturally, I smiled back.

"Uh-oh, sorry, babe. Where's my nephew?"

"Taking a walk. Thanks for the ride home, Auntie." I rotated around her and out the screened door before someone thought up some work for me. I figured I could be with Nick in about five minutes. Smiles was missing out on the fun since Father took him early this morning for new horseshoes at Cousin TeeShirt's place.

Outside, my excitement geysered. I broke into a skip dance whispering, "Oh yeah. Oh yeah. I'm free. Oh yeah."

Splash! Reality can be harsh. This time it hit me like a pan full of dirty potato-peeling water hurling out the back door.

What about *Wol-la-chee*? I hadn't given Him Birdie's other relics yet, and He'd hit the Yazzees with a double whammy this past week. It all spelled danger, and Nick was in the middle of it.

Against my own rule, I gnawed on a scarf knot and stared at the furrowed road in front of me. Lately, I'd shunned Red Rocks and Concho Mountain as if they were rattlesnake resorts. Now something Father mentioned a lot popped into my head.

Father said every road in life had forks in it, and the forks were where you found out about yourself. The forks were really choices. He said we all walk around wearing the choices we make at the forks in our roads.

Hmm. One fork to choose right now was staying here with the women. I'd be safe, bored, and terrified for Nick. Or I could stop being a coward and go find my brother. That was the other fork.

Just Go.

I jumped the short cedar railing by the hogan with a hand-over and raced down the red road. Waste no time, feet. Right foot. Left foot. Foot up. Foot down. I imagined Nick's favorite coach—Mr. Miyagi from the old *Karate Kid* movies—coaching me. Left foot. Right foot. Not far now. Wax on. Wax off. It kept me from screaming.

I cut through a corner of the orchard, then jogged back onto the track. A light eastern wind puffed oven breath in my face. For some reason, my breathing sounded too loud. My feet pounding the dirt was extra noisy too. I slowed, trotted, stopped. Something felt peculiar. My neck hair became sensitive. I took off in a hard run.

Wait a minute…did I hear footsteps besides my own? No. Yes. Maybe. I wasn't sure. That's when I felt it— *something* warm behind my back. Sharp nervous-needles punctured my pores. My throat tightened above my collarbone.

It was the end for me.

"Oh Nick, Nick!" I cried.

Chapter 16
Smoke!

"**Y**ES?" **A DEEP VOICE BOOMED** into the back of my hair. I screamed. Hands raised me off the ground. I kicked my legs and howled with all my might. Slowly, it seeped into my consciousness that Nick was my captor; but I couldn't stop freaking out. He lowered me to the ground. I turned around slapping his chest and arms. He was playing. I wasn't.

"Wow, what a little cougar," Nick said, easily binding both my hands with one of his.

"Sheep Shears, Nick! What'd you do, fall out of the stupid sky?"

"No. I fell…" Nick raised one eyebrow, "…into step behind you at the edge of the orchard. I've been matching you step for step. Well, almost. You run okay—for a girl." He let go of my hands.

Relief began a slow journey upward, starting at my ankles. "Then…that was both of us breathing and…your footsteps… Oh-my-gosh, Nick. You're worse than ol' coyote." I slugged him hard in the arm. In our Navajo world, the coyote is a trickster you dared not trust.

"Oh, I get it. You call me; I answer. Then I get beat up and called a coyote." He shook his head in pretend misery. "It's a sad day on the Rez, sister. Sad."

How did he do it? I felt fantastic again. I threw my head back and laughed at the sky. It was painted tropical blue and dotted with pearly clouds.

It was true—Nick was magical. Even better, he was not *Wol-la-chee*.

My lips felt glued in a smile as we walked toward Red Rocks. "Face it, Nick, you can't beat me to the top of Echo Rock anymore."

"What? I thought I heard a pip squeaking."

"Prepare for defeat, brother."

We positioned to race. The sound of a hawk's penetrating cry lured Nick's eyes upward. I saw my chance. "Go," I whispered, shooting off like a deer late for supper. I headed right and circled the edge of the boulder formation. Velvety rabbitbrush leaves swished against my jeans as I sliced through them.

I suffered a small setback when the sandy passage leading to Lookout Mound avalanched, carrying me backward several feet. I stepped up it again. I willed myself to be as flat as a corncake at the top so I could wiggle through the gap between Brother Boulders. That gained me a few seconds. I sprinted five steps and worked my way up the side of Echo Rock using natural footholds and the branches of a juniper growing from a gorge. I pulled myself over the top to victory.

Nick lounged beside the solitary juniper growing from the crack in the top of Echo Rock. He leaned back on his elbows with his legs stretched out in front of him. He chewed on a twig and scanned the view.

"Nick, how—?"

"Quiet. I'm listening to the wind's important message. 'What's that? Yessir, I will,'" he said, nodding his head. "The wind says you will never beat your brother up the side of these rocks. He said you must stop these foolish quests or you won't be allowed to grow taller."

I crossed the space between us and tried to shake Nick's shoulders. It was like trying to push a car with no wheels. I groaned, but inside, I was singing. I dropped beside him and hugged my knees. I wanted to start right in telling him about the awful Ancient Ant Man and his crazy tricks, but Grandfather said it was important to start a good story at just the right spot. Birdie always accused me of starting my stories from the day the earth was created. Was that bad? I played with the red, white, and blue plaid laces in my tennis shoes and thought about it. In a few minutes, I had it figured out.

"Nick, did you know that ants have —" My sentence stuck in my throat when I looked at Nick. He stared toward the Valley of Remembrance with strange, empty eyes. It was almost like he wasn't Nick, or even human. His brows went together, relaxed, then met again. It scared me. I steepled my hands and rested them against my nose.

Sometimes when I sat cross-legged on Smiles' back, I watched the wind blowing clouds quickly across the enormous Navajo Nation sky. As they passed over, the flickering cloud shadows changed the color and shape of everything below them. That's what was happening to Nick's face right now—troubled clouds blew across his mind.

His face changed from furious to gentle, shocked to sad. Hard. Soft. Worried. Calm.

My eyes filled with tears. The war had injured my brother's spirit, and it was just like him to keep us all laughing while he was suffering inside. I squeezed my eyes shut and made a double-dog important decision. I would remember this day and make it a symbol to my new courage. From now on, I would work hard to be as brave as Nick.

I buried my face in soft scarf folds. Nick's voice startled me.

"I could eat fifteen hamburgers, a mile-high stack of fry bread, and a washtub full of beans, Little Dove."

Nick was back on this earth with me. I wiped my eyes and smiled at him. He lay back and put his head on his arms. A disharmonious sound behind us sent me to the edge of Echo Rock to look down. A flock of Pinion jays had captured a grandfather-sized cedar tree. Their rowdy squawking seemed disrespectful right now. I frowned at them for disturbing our peace.

Something in the distance caught my eye. I visored my hands over my eyes to cut the midday glare. "Nick, smoke at the Tso place!"

"Let's go," he said, leaping to his feet.

We slid off Echo Rock on our rears and flung ourselves the rest of the way down. We ran the half mile to the Tso's in minutes.

"Fire! Fire!" we yelled, leaping the cattle guard and turning in every direction.

"Mr. Tso! Mrs. Tso!" Nick called.

"No one's here," I said. My words sounded hollow in the smoky air. A high-pitched horse squeal and the thud of hooves kicking wood came from inside the smoking shed.

The Tso's didn't have a horse.

"Oh-my-gosh! It's Tito, Nick! He had surgery on his leg a few weeks ago. I have to save him!" I blasted off to rescue Tito, but Nick's voice lassoed me like a short rope on a runaway calf.

"No, let's water down the fire first so it doesn't spread to the pen and the house." Nick shed his maroon T-shirt and flung it across the water pump beside the horse trough. I hesitated, but only for a few seconds. I trusted Nick.

We yanked buckets from the side of the old shed the Tso's were using as their barn. Time passed in flashes. We dipped our buckets in the trough and ran inside to soak the tongues of fire licking the wall and floor. Nick and I coughed on the run. Tito's kicks became more desperate. I called out to him each time I dumped a bucket of water. The thought of Tito perishing in the shed's corner stall was unbearable.

Finally, I dropped my bucket to the ground and wiped my face on Nick's T-shirt. "I'm going after him." Nick fixed me with a severe look before swabbing his face on his forearm.

"You know a scared horse is dangerous, Silki. Tito's spooked real good right now. I'll go get him." He headed in the direction of the shed. I captured Nick's elbow with both hands.

"Tito knows me best, Nick. Please?" I loved Tito. He was part of my life with the *old Birdie*. Nick's eyes narrowed, but he nodded.

I scrubbed black gook off my hands in the water and wiped them down the front of my jeans. I unknotted one of my scarves with shaking hands and dunked it in the water. I squeezed and shook it as I ran toward Tito. I wasn't sure how I'd use it, but ideas were cooking in my brain.

I flipped the latch on the stall door and eased the door open. Tito snorted and reared up two quick times. I stepped backward, pulling the door toward me as far as the hinges would go. Waiting behind it, I prayed Tito would seek his freedom and run outside. He didn't. He backed into the corner breathing noisily. I dropped my wet scarf over the top of the stall door and stepped inside. Time for some girl-to-horse coaxing.

"Hey, Tito, we're buddies, right? Take it easy, now. That's it." He quieted a little hearing a familiar voice. He knew me almost as well as he knew Birdie, but his instincts were on high alert. Too fast, I poked my open hand out for him to smell. His head flew up. His eyes went all crazy, with more white showing than color.

Darn it, Silki!

I should have been more patient. Tito whinnied, kicked the back wall, and flattened his ears. His breathing became louder. With his bared teeth and diamond-shaped nostrils, he was beginning not to look like Tito. I felt woozy watching him lower his head like Cousin TeeShirt's angry rodeo bull did right before he charged. I recognized full-fight mode when I saw it.

Something inside me backed my body out the stall opening. I slammed the door shut as Tito's head butted the boards behind my quaking hands.

"Silki!" Nick yelled from across the floor. I heard the splash of water as he emptied another bucket.

"I'm okay, Nick. I promise. Tito is doing great." I heard Nick say *Holy* something, but I didn't catch the end of it.

I took deep breaths and put my hand on the stall-door latch. This time, I would be patient and gain Tito's trust. Afterward, I'd lead him to safety. How? The halters and ropes were in the corner behind the flames and burned out floor. I looked at my scarf chain, then wound it around my forearm. I stepped into the stall with an air of confidence. Tito snorted a warning and dipped his head. I stood tall, never taking my eyes from his. Once I had his attention, I spread his name around like a warm blanket.

"Tito. What a good Tito you are." I almost wished I knew Birdie's secret name for him because he would have come to me or at least calmed down. Smiles went all soft and buttery when I used his secret name. The rule was no one could know the secret name except the owner and the horse. It was an old Native custom, and it was powerful.

"Be brave, Tito. Pretend I'm Birdie." I soothed him, using movements he was used to seeing. His ears rotated forward a little crookedly, and his neck muscles softened. I walked down them with feathery fingers. He fretted, his flesh quivering. I made sure he could see me every second as I eased my wet scarf onto his back like a saddle blanket. He turned his head to stare at it. I almost laughed at his expression.

"Nice and cool, huh Tito?"

I uncoiled the scarves from my arm. In one smooth move, I threaded them under his neck and over his mane to tie into a loop. Tito and Smiles were used to my scarves; they'd worn them forever.

Holding back my coughs was causing my eyes to drip smoky tears. "Come on, Tito," I said, tugging gently on the scarf rope. He pulled back, then surrendered. I found Nick flattened against the wall just outside the stall—always the warrior ready to rescue. Pride blazed across his face when I passed him leading a meek Tito.

Outside, I coughed from my toes up.

Chapter 17
The Sunglasses

SQUEAKY RED AND WHITE pickup in the middle of a dust ball came down the road and wheezed to a stop. The Tso's spilled from the doors and the back end of the truck. Nick waved his T-shirt like he was scrubbing the air.

I examined Tito's front leg. Most of the stitches were dissolved, but a trickle of blood oozed from a few spots. The Tso family swarmed toward us. I glanced at Nick. He was covered in black grunge. I didn't want to know how I looked. I pushed my hair behind my ears and tugged at the bottom of my blouse.

"*Ya'at'eeh*," Mr. Tso called. The two younger Tso boys, Lee and Eugene, ran toward Tito and me. They chitter-chattered like a cage full of baby chicks.

"Is Tito all right? Look at his leg. Blood! Why is he wearing that pink scarf on his back? What's he doing with all those other scarves around his neck?" I shushed them. Robert, the oldest Tso boy, strolled up smiling at me. He pushed his straw cowboy hat off his forehead and crossed his arms.

"Can you guys back off and let Tito breathe?" I asked. Six legs stepped back in unison.

"I heard you came home, Nick." Mr. Tso said, looking from the half-burned shed to Nick. "Did we have war here too?"

Nick grinned. "Not quite, uncle. Looks like your fire started from that old cord and socket hanging in the feed area. Probably short-circuited, made some sparks. That lit the straw on the floor. It was easy going from there with all those empty gunnysacks on a dry wood floor. Sure a good thing you store your hay and gas over there." Nick pointed to a small open structure with a rusty metal roof. It was stacked with rectangles of hay. A dented gasoline can with a nozzle leaned against a post.

"Mm," Mr. Tso said, pinching his cheek and staring at the burnt shed. "Time to get my boys on some real men's work," he said, jamming his hands into his pockets and raising a booted foot onto the rim of the horse trough.

Tito nickered.

"Looks like my sister made a *clothes horse* out of Tito," Nick teased. Mrs. Tso laughed and slapped her leg.

"Silki, look at me," seven-year-old Lily Tso said, sticking her head out from behind her mother. I gulped in mid-smile. Blue lens sunglasses with painted sunflowers on the sides topped Lily Tso's round smile.

"See?" she said, whipping the glasses off and putting them back on. "I'm a rock star." She ducked behind Mrs. Tso, dropped to her knees, and wrapped chubby arms around her mother's legs.

"Yeah, she found those things somewhere out here last week." Mrs. Tso said, trying to unlock one of Lily's hands from her leg. "Don't know where they came from… the sky I guess." She laughed with gusto. "Can't get them away from her." Mrs. Tso sidestepped. Lily followed on her knees. Mrs. Tso grinned and shrugged her shoulders.

Mr. Tso scratched his temple. His straw cowboy hat rose and fell with each movement of his hand. "Uh-huh. Same day Lily found those glasses, one of my old buckets went walking off. See that wall up there where you got the buckets? Three nails. Now I just got two buckets. Guess that's plenty," he said.

My sunglasses here? A missing bucket?

Mr. Tso took command of his troops. "Robert, hook up the horse trailer and load Tito. Eugene, pour more water inside the shed. Check it real good. Lee, build a fire. I'll bring a brisket back from town."

The creases around Mr. Tso's eyes pinched together when he smiled at Nick and me. *"Ahéhee'.* Both of you. I am grateful. Good thing you came to see us today." He turned toward his truck. "I'm getting my brother Danny to look at that horse's leg. Go right by your outfit. I'll drop you off," he said.

I handed Tito over to a grinning Robert. What was his problem, anyway?

My insides churned as I passed Lily wearing my missing sunglasses. I followed Nick to the truck like a scolded puppy, tucked tail and all.

Chapter 18
Misery and Joy

A T HOME, A FLOOD of people flowed through our yard like rain runoff. Some sat on blankets or rugs spread on the ground. Others leaned against the house or sat in chair circles. Kids climbed in and out of pickup beds and ran as free as chickens through the yard. A buzz of *Diné Bizaad*, English, and low-toned chuckles mixed in with the afternoon air currents.

It all made me mad. Nick hadn't been home twenty-four hours. Couldn't people wait? By the peaceful look on Father's face as he set up chairs, I guessed not.

"Me and Kathleen will be over later," Mr. Tso's gold molar gleamed in the back of his mouth when he grinned. Nick leaned back into the truck to say something. I walked to the back of the trailer to touch Tito's tan coat through the holes in the metal.

"Bye old partner," I said as a huge wave of *sad* rolled over me. I wondered how to keep from dropping in the road and blubbering like a baby. Mr. Tso's trailer surged forward in a mantle of dust. I watched Tito's black tail blowing out the back end until it looked like one of the horsetails in my miniature horse set. Traitor tears ran down my cheeks faster than I could rub them away. All I wanted was for Birdie to be here with me and life to be like it was before. Was that too much to ask?

I turned toward the house. Nick was visiting in a 360-rotation. Boy, did he ever love people. And they loved him back. He already balanced a paper plate loaded with food. How did he get it so fast? Of course, someone fixed it for him. Covered in splashy soot strokes, he looked battle ready—except for his humongous smile and happy eyes. I sketched him in my mind.

I aimed for *invisible* and made my way toward the front door. Father nodded me a glad-you're-here smile. I stood over the two card tables set up in the yard sniffing sliced meats, boiled eggs, zucchini and tomatoes cooked with bacon, salsas, chips, tortillas, pickles, and sliced white bread. Grandmother's covered pot of corn soup rested on potholders beside a stack of Styrofoam bowls and a box of Saltine crackers. It seemed impossible, but I wasn't hungry.

Nick's laugh stole my attention. I rammed into something, and icy water splashed over my waist and down the front of my jeans, turning them indigo blue. I grabbed the top of a teetering metal washtub filled with sloshy ice and drinks. Father's two hands came from nowhere and gripped beside mine. Fred Toledo, a town council member, shot from the ground to steady the barrel underneath the tub.

"Sorry," I whispered, my cheeks frying with embarrassment. So much for being invisible. I couldn't wait to get inside and cry my eyes out. Thanks to *Wol-la-chee* and Birdie, I was turning into a big bawl-bag.

Inside, I jerked the bathroom door toward me as Auntie Jane shoved it from the other side. We screamed, our faces inches apart.

"Goodness gracious, you scared me!" Auntie Jane pressed the tips of her pink polished nails to her lips. Her smile faded. "What in the world…you're a mess!"

I patted my bangs and wiped at my cheeks. "We just put out a fire in the Tso's shed a little while ago."

Auntie Jane's eyes widened. "Is everyone okay?"

"Uh-huh. Mr. Tso said he was going to put Eugene, Lee, and Robert to work building a new shed. Tito was trapped inside, and I saved him. He's on his way to see Danny Tso right now to have his stitches checked. He had surgery a few weeks ago, you know. I can tell he's lonely. Birdie shouldn't leave him like that. I know you agree with me. Anyway, Nick's outside wearing his war paint and running for President of the Universe I think," I said, all in one breath.

"You sure can rattle it off with the big boys when you want to, babe." Auntie Jane smiled and shook her head. I smiled back. She moved around me in a wide loop. "Hurry on in there," she said, pointing to the bathroom and backing away. "There you go. I'll just get out of the way and let you do your little cleanup. You said Nick is…?" she pointed outside.

"Right outside the door, Auntie. You can't miss him."

"Right." She smiled and pinkie-finger waved good-bye before hurrying down the hall. Auntie Jane had a steroid hatred of dirt. It sort of ran in the family. At least she didn't scrub the grain off our wood floors like my Auntie Blue Corn tried to do on her visits.

I felt better after cleaning up. I claimed a place on our concrete porch next to the terracotta pot growing Father's special habanero peppers. I gathered my knees under my chin and checked out the clamor around me. Grandmother came from around the side of the house wearing a scarf and carrying a heavy pot of something. Two women rose to help her. A makeshift table of an old door lying across two sawhorses had shown up while I was inside. It was already crowded with pots, bowls, jars, and baskets. Nick, or course, was group hopping and eating.

Not talking, I heard a lot.

Alice Perez's daughter got engaged to an Anglo doctor from New Mexico. Alice didn't like her only child leaving the Rez, so she expected free Tylenol for life from the arrangement. As soon as she said the Tylenol part, her shoulders heaved up and down in silent laughter.

A new high school principal and tax issues were on the next agenda at the Chapter House. According to Mr. Toledo, it was high time the politicians in Washington fulfilled their latest promises to *Dinéteh*. Or any promises, for that matter.

Two widowed sisters in their mid-eighties, Clara Sapp and Cora Redhouse, chatted about a serious crime near Rattlesnake they'd read about in the *Navajo Times*. As soon as they started telling the details, Father rose from his chair clearing his throat. "Coffee?" he asked. That was my dad's way—he wanted conversations to stay light, especially when I was around.

Grandfather brought up the subject of changing weather patterns, but Uncle Bennie sideswiped the conversation with a loud, "We need the old ways."

Uncle Bennie was more or less deaf from an Army jeep accident in his twenties. People smiled good-naturedly when he wandered into their conversations and took over. In a voice unusually loud by Navajo standards, Uncle Bennie said his dogs had been barking him awake at night. And someone took his favorite skinning knife and a box of kitchen matches out of his tool shed—someone who just should have asked first.

I gasped. *Wol-la-chee* stealing randomly?

Just then, a whirlwind drove down the road from the direction of town. When the sand settled, a blue, old-model Buick LeSabre convertible with Nick's friends popping out of the top sat in front of our house. Most of Nick's former high school basketball team jumped out of it.

Nick tore out to meet them. They moved to his trailer like a wad of paper people hot-glued together. Everyone grinned when they passed. Then the visiting murmurs resumed.

Later, guy hoots and challenges—along with the *whoomf* of Nick's basketball bouncing off firm ground—squeezed through the wire screen of my open window until late. Both misery and joy rained over me in gusts.

Wol-la-chee messing up my life—misery.

Nick would *poof!* and be gone in just a few days—double misery.

The happiness in Nick's voice tonight—total joy.

Chapter 19
A Good Trade

T HE ONE THING MOTHER cooked that was 1) edible, and 2) actually delicious, was scrambled eggs. She said the scrambled eggs she fixed in her dorm room in college saved her life. I hoped I never owed my life to eggs. It just didn't seem right.

At breakfast, I was careful to save room for a funnel cake at the parade. Nick ate tortillas and Mother's eggs mixed with pieces of Jimmy Dean sage sausage and Grandmother's jalapeño relish until I felt sick. Maybe it was true what Grandfather said—Nick had hollow legs to store all that food he ate.

Father dubbed me the official meat griller for our Big Eat tomorrow and said I should start grilling right after the parade. Nick grabbed his throat and made gagging noises. While I ground my bare heel into the top of his boot under the table, Mother lapsed into one of her dramatic moods.

Using expressive hand gestures like teachers use, she said, "The Fourth of July scoops up our people from hidden corners of the Navajo Nation and sets them down metaphorically in a particular place like Dorothy in *The Wizard of Oz*. In that way, celebratory situations are not unlike tornadoes."

Whatever, Mother.

What I knew was that the celebrations gave Grandfather a chance to jaw with his old veteran buddies and tell everyone and their animals why they should support the Code Talker Museum. It also gave him a chance to show off his latest high-tech gadget or CD.

Grandmother used celebrations to catch up on Rez gossip and news. Her bait was food, and everyone came around to sample her *atoo'*, specialty grilled meats, fry bread, beans, and homemade salsas and relish. That had been true forever. What hadn't been true forever was me—without Birdie.

Two things ruined the parade for me: 1) Geri from Resources in the high school library introduced me to a new friend of hers. Watching them talk and laugh made me extra lonely for mean old Birdie, and 2) Robert Tso pranced by on Tito. His big, showy wave in my direction almost made me throw up.

Later, some girls from Birdie's and my old dance troupe asked me to go on carnival rides with them. I didn't feel like it—not even my favorite ride, the *Zipper*. I was a one-best-friend kind of girl anyway. Not like Nick and his crowd of followers.

Back home, I gathered up the glass pans of marinated ribs, fixed myself a quart jar of ice and tea and sludged over to Grandmother's. I had to grill at her house so she could add more seasoned meats all afternoon.

I stared at the smoke floating like a ghost over the racks of ribs. The mesquite smell teased my stomach into growling, but I ignored it. I'd felt yucky since yesterday at the Tso's. This summer of the Ancient was making me sick. I desperately needed to share my secrets with someone, especially Nick. But how could I ruin his last few days at home after I saw the suffering behind his smiles?

I rotated the ribs with metal tongs and Grandmother's bone-handled fork her mother gave her about a thousand-million years ago. I straddled the pine bench under the arbor and brushed a fly off my arm. My head clunked to the table.

So much didn't make sense—like Lily finding my sunglasses out by the Tso's shed. Maybe I'd see my missing tangerine scarf flying from a flagpole at the fairgrounds tomorrow. Or we might hear about Mother's hand sanitizer showing up in someone's ice chest. If the Tso's missing bucket materialized on top of Robert's head the next time he mounted Tito, that would be just fine.

I took a swig of tea and let my head fall back to the table. Where was crazy Birdie anyway? I hadn't seen her or any of the Yazzees today. Before Birdie's mutation into my Evil Friend, she told me her dumb volleyball camp was done before the Fourth of July.

She used to say Nick was her older brother too, but she hadn't called to say *hi* or check on him since he came home. I'd saved her beautiful horse from fire and brimstone yesterday. Didn't she love Tito enough to call about him? Maybe if he looked more like a volleyball?

Grandmother's head popped out the door. "Silki, don't go to sleep. Need more cumin for the chops. Hurry." I didn't hurry. When my think-and-drag-feet moods hit me, I moved like a centipede in leg casts.

I stepped through our kitchen door and wished I could zoom back out. Boxes. Bags. Spices. Spills. Every surface littered with pans, dishes, and chopped food. When Mother cooked—which wasn't often, thank goodness—she reminded me of a dazed octopus. How could one perfectly organized professor make such a mess in the kitchen?

I fished the cumin can from the spice shelf and attempted an escape. Too late.

"Can you bring some chilies from Grandmother's?" Mother blew a piece of hair out of her eyes. "Mercy!" she said, lifting a saucepan off a gas burner. Something smelled burnt.

"Grab that bowl for me," she ordered. I held a gold and white Pyrex bowl under the pan while Mother dumped the whatever-it-was into it. Black goo covered the bottom of the pan. "Well, would you look at that," Mother said.

"Be back," I garbled, taking man-sized steps to freedom.

Once inside the hogan, it struck me that something didn't seem right. I backed out the door and glanced at the fire pit. The grill was empty. A lopsided hat sat a few feet away.

The *Wol-la-chee* shuffle again?

I ran to look for footprints around the pit. Nothing but an oil drill could have left an imprint in that rock-hard stuff. How long had I been at my house—four or five minutes? I ran around the hogan two times. Nothing. I looked down the road. Maybe *Wol-la-chee* was invisible, but our meat wasn't. The idea of two racks of ribs floating through the air toward Concho Mountain was more than I could take.

"Aghhh!" I yelled, grabbing my head and jumping up and down on one foot. That was my version of going nuts for a few seconds.

Maybe Grandmother took the ribs inside.

Sure, and Clint Eastwood left his cowboy hat by the fire pit?

Is it possible to have a sarcastic fight with yourself? I think so.

I slogged inside and put the red and white cumin can on the counter. I stepped away with my arms Velcroed to my sides. I watched Grandmother shake cumin into a bowl of mostly red dry stuff and stir it with a fork. She peeled chops off a glazed platter and dragged them through the rub, pressing with her fingers.

"I don't see any ribs in here," I said, in a whiney voice. Grandmother tossed me a sour look and continued massaging pork pieces.

Not good enough. I had to know what happened to those ridiculous ribs. Android-like, I said, "The...ribs... are...where...Grandmother?" Her shoulders rose in a sigh. She rinsed her hands and scavenged an oblong cake pan from under the sink. I robotically followed her out the door. I knew she thought I was a pain.

Grandmother stopped midway under the arbor and looked between the empty grill and the hat. Maybe *Wol-la-chee's* Hour of Revelation had come at last.

Without unsealing her gaze, Grandmother slid the pan onto the pine table. Hands on her hips, she took tiny steps toward the hat. I figured that deep river Grandfather talked about was flooding her mind and making it a little hard for her to walk at the same time.

After a long five minutes or so, she picked up the hat and read the inside label. In her own good time, she blew off the dust and started remodeling the smashed part. She placed it on her head and smoothed the brim with her fingertips. She turned toward me with a satisfied, curvy-S smile on her lips.

"A Stetson. Pretty good trade, Silki." She passed me and my open mouth on her way back inside.

Was I dreaming? I sank onto the bench feeling dazed and crazed. I couldn't believe my grandmother's reaction. Nobody understood what was happening on the Rez this summer. How long could I be The Keeper of such a terrible secret?

Deep inside, a volcano puffed angry smoke into my spirit. I was sick of fear. I was worn-out missing Birdie. Mostly, I was *bá ntseeshdá* with *Wol-la-chee* ruining my life. I belonged here. He didn't.

A plan began clotting in what our biology teacher called *Wetware*—my brain. What if I went to Concho Mountain and confronted Him? What if I gave every stinking piece of old history back and ordered Him to leave? Was that normal thinking—me hashing it out with an Ancient Being that almost didn't exist?

Maybe not normal, but definitely brave. After all, *the new Silki* was bursting with courage, right?

Chapter 20
Weird Relief

OKAY, NEVER MIND THE NOON HEAT made me feel like a fried egg with legs traipsing up and down rows of vehicles looking for Mother's truck. So what if nine out of ten of the vehicles in the parking field were pickup trucks and not cars? Did it matter if every vehicle out there wore a matching dust robe from a harsh but short sandstorm that passed through earlier this morning?

No. Why not? Because Grandmother had spoken.

She told me, "You have a good sense of direction. You'll find it." Before I could ask her what a sense of direction had to do with finding one single truck in a sea of trucks, she waved me away.

All of this for two jars of pepper relish, green onions, lettuce, and a bag of ice.

It wasn't like I had anything else to do on the *Big Eat* day. I was now best-friend-less, and the town elders had hijacked my brother for a ceremony.

I wiped my damp forehead on my arm. It would have helped if I'd come with Mother this morning, but I'd ridden with Auntie Jane and Grandfather. Now Mother was off some place voicing her opinion with the Tribal Council or judging dancers or who knew what. That was my mother's way.

A few seconds before I became an ex-human and melted into a bio-spot on the trampled fairground dirt, I spotted the ice blue, double-cab Dodge with tinted windows and vinyl-coated truck bed—my mother's new pride and joy. I'd never seen it so filthy, but it matched all the other trucks, SUVs, and cars that had gone through the sandstorm.

Coming up on the passenger side, I heard Father's voice from the other side of the cab. He and someone else were leaning with their backs against the driver's window. I stepped up on the rear bumper and waited for a break in their conversation. It was worth a short wait to get Father's help lugging the ice chest back to the picnic area.

I sat down on the edge of the tailgate and daydreamed of jumping, clothes and all, into the cold pool at the Canyon Recreation Center. I imagined the chilly liquid seeping up to my ear lobes. My cool mirage disappeared with Father's voice.

"Bad business, Jake. Anyone else hurt?" he asked.

"No, just Officer Dele. But he's doing pretty good now. He fired one good shot. They found blood outside the pawn store. Guy got away, though."

"I hate to hear stuff like that," Father said.

"I know what you mean, Frank. I thought you heard about it already. It happened last month."

"No, I was real busy with shipments. You know, I think catalogs and the Internet are going to work pretty good for my jewelry business."

A break in their talking stretched so long, I started to say something. Father beat me to it.

"You know, I'm a little like a turtle, Jake. I stick my head out sometimes. If the news out there is good, I stay and soak up some sun. If it's bad, I go back in my shell awhile." Father and the other man laughed. Father continued.

"You guys see a lot more ugly stuff than the rest of us. Just the business you're in." They shifted, and I saw a holster and bullets. Father's talking partner was Lt. Jake, a Navajo Nation police officer.

"That's right," Lt. Jake said. "Part of the territory. We hear it all. Like a few weeks ago, my cousin Rollie—he's a cop up by Shiprock. Anyway, a man up around there got clobbered in the head in his own house. Real bad too. Put him in a coma."

I gasped. That sounded like the story Clara and Cora brought up a few days ago.

"Don't know what happened to his boy—think he was about sixteen. Can't remember what Rollie said. A minor anyways. He just up and disappeared," Lt. Jake said. "You just don't know these days, do you?"

"Wow. Bad medicine." Father turned to slam his hand on the truck roof to show his disgust. His eyes grew three sizes when he saw me perched on the tailgate.

"Oh, Silki. You been sitting there long?"

"Nuh-uh, Dad. I just got here," I fibbed. My father would feel awful if he thought I overheard his man-talk. He still thought I was too young for stuff like that. He didn't realize we studied about war and violence in our history classes.

Anyway, after dealing with a slippery character like *Wol-la-chee* the past few weeks, it was a weird relief to hear nitty-gritty crime stories with real humans.

"What are you doing out here in the heat instead of the shade, honey?"

"Just making Grandmother happy, Dad," I said, pointing at the ice chest.

"Jake, I'm raising a real intelligent girl here," Father said, grinning at the policeman and reaching for the white container.

Chapter 21
Trouble at the Tent

MOTHER'S HANDS WERE LIKE ceiling fans ready to spin. With fuchsia sticky strips stuck to all ten of her spread fingers, I knew to duck. Another row of strips decorated the side of her Levi vest beside the buttonholes. Nothing but brainstorming about more projects could have done this to her.

The dreamy expression on her face and the angle of her raised eyebrow sent me scooting off the picnic bench and onto the ground blanket behind Father's back. Mother peeled the little scribbled papers off and stuck them to the top of the picnic table.

"Oh, Frank." she breathed. She shook her head and closed her eyes as if she'd just leaned back in the perfect bubble bath. "Frank. Frank. It is so impossible to evaluate the margin of error when opportunities are either salvaged, or lost forever if not seized in that last fragment of possibility."

Oh-my-gosh. What had Mother been up to this time?

"Uh-huh," Father said, nodding. He went to lean against the table in front of her. Without him shielding me, I felt exposed to Mother's educational radiation.

"If Delores and I had lingered five more minutes inside the exhibit hall, we wouldn't have run into Dr. Gavriel—of the Smithsonian Institute, Frank! Can you imagine if he'd put one foot into that black Hummer before we saw him..." Mother's voice droned on.

Whoosh. No telling what test-rat stuff would come of this. Maybe I should just will my body to science right now and get it over with. I blew a stream of air into the sky and fell back onto the geometric designs of one of Grandmother's rugs. Background carnival racket and distant drumbeats burrowed under my skin like ticks. I was restless. And irritated.

How long could one stupid Sunday be anyway? It was strange to feel so alone with people everywhere. Eva Binwa asked me earlier if I wanted to hang out with her and her cousins to ride carnival rides. I didn't. I hated to admit it, but sweating over Mother's language project tomorrow sounded pretty good. Anything was better than feeling the hole Birdie had poked in my heart.

Narrowing my eyes to stare through my eyelash hairs made the Ferris wheel circling the dusk sky bleed into hazy streaks. Maybe that's how my life was this summer—blurry blobs of color. I moaned and flipped onto my side.

Now where did Mother go? Father was talking to two men. An ornate golden leather drum bag with fringe so long it swept the ground draped his left shoulder. That meant he was headed to the men's tent where the musicians and dancers hung out between performances.

Where was the rest of my family? I knew Auntie Jane was helping the ROAR folks find homes for homeless Rez animals. That was one of her big things. Auntie Zim and Jesse were spending the day together at the carnival and rodeo. I spied Grandmother and other elders in a semi-circle of mismatched folding chairs next to the bleachers. Grandfather stood in front of the flock demonstrating something with arm movements. When he finished, everyone laughed. For no reason at all, their laughter annoyed me.

From the corner of my eye, I saw Father walk away from the men. What the...? Was twilight playing tricks on my eyes? I strained to see. Mother's sticky strips were plastered all over the seat of Father's black Wranglers. I guessed he sat down on them while he was listening to Mother's outburst.

Just like that, it became my Mission of the Night to save my dad from humiliation.

I jumped up and followed him, swiveling through the crowd. The washed-out blues and pale yellows of the lights lining the carnival rides cast sunken shadows on the faces I passed. People's casual strolling frustrated me. Smells of popcorn and fried foods were sickening.

I almost tripped over a young boy who stepped out in front of me wearing a hideous Batman Joker mask. I blasted him with a stern frown. He teetered backward laughing and holding his stomach. It felt like I was in an alternate universe.

Father stopped to talk to a man a few feet from the rear opening of the pole tent Mr. Tsosie was letting the male musicians and dancers use this year. I'd noticed its wide red and white stripes rising in double peaks earlier when I stood on the picnic table. It looked like a circus tent, but Grandfather said Mr. Tsosie's nephew used it for hotsy-totsy business meetings. For the first time—the men, at least—didn't have to change clothes in portable toilets or in their own vehicles. Father said that was creating a lot of good talk.

The weak glow from a few bulbs dangling from cords wrapped around electrical wires barely lit the backside of the tent. Dancers in complicated performance regalia swarmed like fancy-dancy wasps outside The Nest Hotel. They practiced skip steps, two steps, and dramatic clockwise swirls with one bent leg and the other leg extended like a clam's locomotion foot.

Soft night breezes whirred with conversation, humming, and muffled warm-up flute sounds drifting from the tent. This was definitely *Man's Land*, and I had no business being in it. I pinched a scarf knot for reassurance and took a step toward Father.

"Silki, *Ya'at'eeh*."

I coiled toward the voice with my pulse racing.

"Hey, it's me, Robert."

Robert was tall. He looked down at me with enough jingle bells on his waist, legs, and ankles to be a living Christmas sleigh. In the muted light from the bulbs, I barely recognized him. Fringe swirled up and down his white leather dance clothes. Feathers shot straight up from a bristled headpiece. He shook one of his legs, relished the sound, and grinned at me.

I didn't feel one bit friendly. I wanted to shout, *Buzz off, wasp!* But I didn't.

"You here to watch me dance tonight?" he asked.

Oh, brother.

"Um, well, I need to…" My one eye wired to Father's back saw him dip inside the tent opening. "Later, Robert." I waffled through the men with a faraway expression, as if I were looking for someone who was just around the next person.

On which side were the drummers sitting? I sneaked along the dark side of the tent, tripping all the way to the ground on a metal rod flaring from somewhere on the canvas. I picked myself up, took about three steps, and fell on another one. After that, I expected the stupid things.

Why was I doing this? It was more than just boredom egging me on. It was like I was uncorking a bottle and all the troubled *Wol-la-chee* liquid was pouring out and I couldn't stop it no matter what. A thrilling craziness pulled me like a magnet.

I dropped and crawled under the tent canvas. I found myself underneath a long table with metal H-shaped legs.

A blue plastic tablecloth hung about two feet off the top of the table. Another table with a red plastic tablecloth bumped up to the one I was hiding under.

A solid hedge of human legs—bare or wrapped in leather, feathers, fringe, bells, and beads—lined up along the table fronts. I struggled to see around them. I spotted Father on the front side of the tent unloading his painted hand drum and fanciest beaded drumsticks. His backside silhouette showed tabs sticking out in all directions.

Why didn't somebody tell him about it? Auntie Jane told me men didn't say anything to each other about clothes tags sticking out or open zippers. She was right. What was wrong with them?

If I could get Father's attention, I'd use sign language to tell him he was about to be nominated to the Hall of Shame. Then I'd melt away with my little danger thrill tucked under my belt. Of course, he would talk to me later about going to the men's tent, but it would be worth it. Father was never very harsh.

The legs packed in tighter by the second. I couldn't see Father now, and I knew he'd never notice me behind the leg wall. I'd have to go to him. How? I tapped my fingers on the floor looking at the dancewear stowed under the table. Each item had a little paper square with a permanent-inked name straight-pinned to it.

Oh-my-gosh. Any minute, someone might stick his head under the table looking for something. What would I say? *Ya'at'eeh—may I help you find your dance outfit?* Scary.

I couldn't just pop out and make my way through all those guys. Maybe I could borrow a piece of headgear for a few minutes so nobody would know I was a girl. I wouldn't hurt it, and…

Silki, you are toto-loco. You know dance outfits are considered sacred by their owners.

Oh, yeah. I knew that. Okay, plan B. When in trouble, look to the scarves. My stomach rolled with excitement. Peril was so much fun. I unknotted two scarves and shaped them like one of the pieces on the floor. Using stray straight pins, I attached my creation to a red scarf with a black bear in the center. I tied the red scarf around my head and let the ends hide my face. I tucked my scarf chain underneath my shirt and blew off how lumpy it looked.

At this point, there were two of me—the one doing this crazy thing, and the second one watching in shock.

A slight gap in the leg line was my opportunity. I popped up among the bodies. Someone's bonnet of choky plumes immediately smashed me in the face. I spit out feathery wisps and swabbed my tongue with my open hand. Gagger.

I tried to turn facing the front of the tent like the other dancers, but something had me trapped. I leaned forward, and my bonnet spilled partway off my head. I grabbed it. I saw a hefty teen's belly trapping my scarf ends against the table. Keeping my chin low on my chest, I tapped him. He tipped to the side and freed me. I straightened my bonnet.

The single line of dancers thickened to about three bodies wide. How many guys could fit in one area? Too many. I felt like I was drowning in a lake of feather and leather.

Tight spaces did unusual things to me. I needed air. A few smothering minutes later, I decided a head examination would help. Speaking of heads, maybe I'd suffered a concussion and needed a hospital. What sticky strips on Father's behind? Probably I hallucinated all that—after the head injury, that is. One thought began to top all others—escape!

I squirmed until my body faced the table again. Now all I had to do was break through the body tangle and drop to the floor. I raised my shoulders and slammed downward with all my might. Nothing happened. I drilled toward the floor until my eyes bugged. In the middle of a burning strain, the dancer's line chugged forward. My feet lifted off the ground. My upper body slid across the tabletop. Orange cheese puffs in a saggy bag were a few stinky inches from my nose. A jar of blimp-sized dill pickles and a fat cylinder of beef jerky book-ended my face.

Music and shrill chanting erupted in the mouth of the tent, drowning out the din of talk surrounding me. Drumbeats invited the bulky rows of dancers to sway like one long Chinese dragon. What if their rhythm crushed me?

A gunnysack shot from the dance line onto the table. With dizzying speed, a feather-covered appendage scraped snack-sized chip bags and candy bars into the sack. A first-aid kit disappeared. More candy. I blinked. Something about the pattern and black and white color of the feathers made me lightheaded. It just couldn't be—*Wol-la-chee* doing his mischief in the men's tent?

My hands clamped onto the edge of the table. I let the strength of terror push my feet through to the floor. I kept the energy going until I curved all the way down and under the table.

The line shuffled forward a few inches. A lumpy burlap sack dragged the ground beside ornately decorated human-looking feet. I crawled on all fours under the two tables with my eyes glued on the sack. Did *Wol-la-chee* follow me here?

I closed my eyes. Smiles and I loped across the golden silk dunes of Arabia. Our hair blew in magnificent swirls—

Snap out of it, Silki!

My serious pledge to be as brave as Nick meant I had to do something. Okay—it was showdown time. I timed my movements. Crawl. Crawl. One. Two. Three. I gushed from the end of the second table like a waterspout and twisted my body to stare straight into my tormentor's face. Only that's not what happened. Everything spun around before the ground rose to greet me. I splattered, stomach-first.

Faces floated around me. Especially Father's. Worry creases lined his forehead. "Silki? What are you doing here?" he asked.

I scrambled into a sitting position. Way too many male eyes stared at me. I scanned them. No one looked anything like the Ancient Ant Man. It was hard to speak with my wind knocked out. I wet my lips and motioned Father to come close so I could whisper in his ear.

"You tripped? Oh, that's too bad, honey. Huh? Really?" Father reached behind and pulled a handful of pink sticky strips off his rear end. His face broke into a giant grin. "Well, bust my old britches. How about that?" Father chuckled, looking around at wide smiles.

I squeezed my father's arm and backed into the crowd. I was completely embarrassed, but furious too. No way had I tripped. I was pushed.

Adrenaline clawed at my empty stomach as I crossed the fairground.

Chapter 22
The Postcard

SANDSTONE PINK SCREEN with black words
blurred in front of my face. I was too close to
the computer monitor, but it didn't matter. How
could I study after a run-in with *Wol-la-chee* last night?
He actually pushed me! I got mad all over again. At least I
knew He wasn't Navajo—He was way too rude.

The high school library had a fourth of its usual
amount of students. I stole looks at their waxy expressions.
Bookworms. Regular people were out celebrating the last
three days of the Fourth of July activities. Not Mother.
Oh no—she was offering extra credit to any student who
stopped by her come-and-go classes today.

Something clamped over my eyes and mouth. Hands!
I screamed uselessly into one of them and squirmed like
a trapped worm. The hand over my eyes lifted, and a face
dropped down in front of mine. It had crossed eyes and a
goofy grin.

"Nick!" I twisted out of my chair with fists. "What is wrong with you?" I said through clenched teeth.

"Shhh. You'll bother all the real students." He said *real* as if he knew what a fake student I'd been all morning. I scolded him with my expression. He laughed, flipped a chair backward, and sat down facing me. I eased back into my chair.

"I thought you and Father went to the art and jewelry show at the exhibit hall," I said.

"Two hours were plenty." He yawned and stretched. "Besides, I want to meet your friend."

He meant Geri. He saw me with her during the parade Friday when he drove by in a car with other veterans and military guys. Later, he called her a *babe*. I was a little jealous of someone stealing his attention so soon, but I got over it. Nick had tons of friends, including females. Nothing serious. Besides, no one could be his sister but me.

I glanced over at Geri. She was talking on her cell phone by the research computer station across the room. "Come outside," I said. I shoved everything into my backpack and lifted it onto my shoulder in case The Great Pest wanted to steal something else from me.

Outside, the heat shimmered off the concrete and slapped our cheeks pink. I fanned my face with the bottom loop of my scarf chain. "Nick, take it easy. I've only known Geri a few weeks."

"Is she related to any of our clans?"

"I don't think so."

"Excellent," Nick smiled. Traditionally, Navajos didn't date or marry anyone from their own clans.

"How old she is?" Nick squenched his eyes tight and waited for my answer.

"Eighteen."

Nick made a fist, pulled his forearm down in front of his face and blew a gusher of air through his front teeth. "Oo-rah," he breathed.

Wow. Nick was sure making a big deal over just one girl.

"So, what's the problem? Let's get back in there and say *Ya'at'eeh*."

"I don't know her very well, Nick. And if I say anything about family, she gets sad. She gets embarrassed real easy too. "

"Don't worry. Just intro your big brother and I'll take it from there. I'm not a mean guy, you know." Loneliness peeked from behind Nick's smile.

That got to me. I knew what *lonely* felt like. I surrendered. Anyway, Nick could talk me into painting my head blue if he wanted to.

"One catch," I said. "Find out about that design she paints on her fingernail. It looks like a fancy shamrock in the middle of white feathers. I'm just curious."

"Deal." We touched our thumbs in the air.

Inside, Geri was back at the Resources counter talking to two teenagers. She pointed to an aisle, and the girls headed that way. Nick and I strolled by as if we were on our way somewhere else.

"*Ya'at'eeh*, Geri," I said.

"Oh, *Ya'at'eeh*, Silki."

I shot her a quick thumbs up for using our *Diné* greeting. "My brother, Nick," I said, patting his shoulder.

Geri's green eyes brightened. She extended a hand with a perfect French manicure. So Californian. They started talking to one another.

Forgotten, I went back to the media table. Before I sank into the chair, I heard Geri's tinkling laugh. Nick had already charmed her.

Well. Here was another chapter in my book of *The Most Bizarre Summer of My Life*. Imagine me, Silki, introducing my big brother to a pretty girl. How many *firsts* could I go through in just a few weeks?

On the way home, Mother questioned me about her test project and said she wasn't going back to school this afternoon.

"So you and Deloris are going to the exhibit hall?" I asked. Deloris was my mom's best friend and a math professor.

"I've had enough celebration, haven't you? I think I'll just, you know, hang out this afternoon," she said. *Waiting for Nick* is what she didn't say.

At home, I skipped straight from the front door out the kitchen door. I craved my horse. Smiles and I had been inseparable ever since Auntie Jane drove up with him in her horse trailer two years ago. Only my auntie and I knew why Smiles was so gorgeous—his dad was an exotic Arabian horse. She said it was best if we didn't advertise that.

Today, we would explore Canyon Daacha for strange treasures. Grandfather said that canyon held many secrets, and I believed him. I never knew what I'd find in its sandy layers, or just lying on the ground. After that, Smiles and I would search Manuelito's Wash for fossils and sugar rocks before galloping home in a fiery apricot sunset. I felt happier by the moment.

I stopped in my tracks. Sheep Shears! I'd forgotten Grandmother's orders on the way home from the fairgrounds last night. She said I had to help her collect emergency dyestuff so she could finish weaving Auntie Zim's wall hanging. Oh, hooray—bending, cutting, digging, and hauling heavy bags in the afternoon heat would be laugh-out-loud fun. Just like that, my great mood kerplunked all the way down to China.

Smiles was prancing excitedly at the gate. I couldn't look him in the eyes. I turned back to the house with five-pound weights pulling my face down. A dusty maroon car edged away from the front of our house.

"What did Carlene want?" I asked Mother inside the house.

"Oh, she was mailing a package at the post office and picked up our mail for us. You have a postcard." She handed it to me. "From Birdie."

Birdie? My heart skipped a beat. I looked at the colored postcard advertising Mrs. Anna's store in Santa Fe. Birdie's tiny scrawling filled up the blank space on the back.

Dear Silki, My Nali got me at volleyball camp erley so I could be with her the 4th. She is lonely since Grandpa Pete you know what last year. I didn't tell you I was going becuse I didn't know I was going when I left Mond. Were you look for me at the parade? My family went to Canyon da Shay with my uncle Shilah. I heard about the blankets and terquoise. Weird. I'm sorry I was so mad at you. I'll call when I get home. Probley on Mond. or Tuesd. Birdie.

A tear smeared some of Birdie's misspelled words. More fell on my hand. Grandmother's light tap on the kitchen door sent me flying out to hug her.

Chapter 23

Grandmother Fiercely

WE WORKED UNTIL GRANDMOTHER said, "Too hot. Let's go." I had to admit our gathering was kind of fun this time. Grandmother's mood since Nick came home was bordering on giddy. Wearing her new-old Stetson hat, she even cracked a few strange jokes while we worked.

We gathered on the low Twin I foothills close to the peach orchard. To stay calm so close to Concho Mountain, I reasoned that, so far, *Wol-la-chee* had been to the high school, our place, Birdie's outfit, the Tso's, Uncle Bennie's, and the men's tent last night. Why should He be on Concho Mountain today? He was probably far away terrorizing other innocent people, I told myself over and over. Once I thought I felt mystic eyes boring into my back, but Grandmother and I were already well down the track toward home by then.

Under the summer arbor, we dumped our two heavy bags and a full bucket onto the grass mat with plenty of *ahhs.* Mother strolled down the path toward us carrying a plastic pitcher and three red and white Solo glasses. She had on white jeans and a blue striped shirt with white cuffs and collar. She looked cool and un-busy. I loved it.

"Let me see what you guys got," she said, walking alongside the table. Unloading our finds with my mom watching made me feel proud for some reason. She named each thing as we unloaded our plastic zip bags. "Three-leaved sumac, lichen, sagebrush, chamizo, rabbitbrush, juniper twigs, berries…"

I turned my gathering bag upside down and shook out dirt and weed stalks. Something else fluttered to the mat. I squatted to have a look. The old photo Birdie found on her porch swing. Why was it in my bag?

Hmm…I had to reason this out. Birdie came the day I washed Smiles. Later, I took her relics out of my pocket and stashed them in the old cigar box. I had a mental image of finding the old photo in my other pocket and sailing it in the air toward my desk. Either it landed in my gathering bag at the end of the desk, or it blew in that night while I had my window open.

Good. Great. Nothing strange about it. I wasn't in the mood for any more *unexplainables.* I stood up and stretched my back, sliding the photo onto the pine table. I swigged lemonade down my parched throat and watched Grandmother drop a bundle of roots into a basket by the door. She took one of Grandfather's red hankies out of her skirt pocket and blotted her forehead.

"Getting as old as *Dookoosliid*," she said, referring to one of our four sacred mountains. She balanced her Stetson hat carefully on a nail above the root basket and accepted a cool drink from Mother. Her eyes crinkled into a smile above the glass. As I said, Grandmother was a new Navajo since Nick came home.

She sat her glass down on the table and winced when she noticed she'd put it on top of a photo. I opened my mouth to explain it didn't matter, but Grandmother grabbed up her drink and slid the picture down her skirt so quick I didn't get a chance.

"Excuse me," she said, grinning. For some reason, a bad feeling came over me.

Grandmother held the picture up and studied it. Her smile turned into a wide-eyed stare. The picture dropped from her hand. A low moan traveled from somewhere deeper than her throat. Her hands curled into fists. She shot out of the yard headed toward Towering Cliff.

"Grandmother!" I shouted. She didn't even slow down. I was afraid she was having a stroke. "What happened to her, Mother?" Mother looked bewildered. She bent and picked up the photo. "I'm going after her," I said. Mother's cool hand on my arm stopped me.

"You don't understand, Silki. She'll be back after she walks her worries awhile. She's...well, surprised. Where did you get this—?"

For some reason, my mouth went AWOL. "What don't I understand? What does this picture have to do with her? Who is that man? Is he our family? Why can't…"

My mother's expression stopped my ranting. Her eyes imprisoned me until my face burned hot. I had interrupted my mother, and rudely. In our *Diné* culture, that was a seriously improper thing to do. Mother turned and slowly walked up the path toward our house.

I stood trembling.

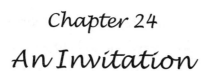

Chapter 24

An Invitation

ICK AND MOTHER'S LAUGHTER in the kitchen sounded offbeat to my mood when I stepped inside our house. I'd been sobbing into Smiles' mane for the past hour.

Before that, I'd tried all my old ways to feel better. I identified birdcalls. That got old fast. I tried using *scarf medicine*. I threaded my blue scarf covered in gold crowns and navy blue stars into the headstall of Smiles' bridle, over his head, and down the other side. I twisted and fluffed until he looked like a palace horse in the Royal Guard. But it was no use.

I gave up and cried rivers of tears. I needed a friend so badly. My only hope was that Birdie was back from Santa Fe.

While I gave Smiles a light brushing, I wondered if Nick was home. Now I knew he was. Hearing their conversation, I didn't think Mother sounded upset about what happened earlier. I still was. Our phone rang. I answered it.

"*Ya'at'eeh*, Silki," Auntie Zim said. "You're the reason I called."

"*Ya'at'eeh*, Auntie." I tried to hide my disappointment that she wasn't Birdie.

"Think you could use a day off tomorrow?" she asked.

"You guys don't need me to help with Jesse?"

"I'm not going to my accounting classes tomorrow. It's fine; I'm a little ahead in my workbook. Your Auntie Jane and I have to help your grandmother cook. I'm fixing more puddings, and maybe an extra cake or two. We don't want your mother going too loco in the kitchen, do we?" Auntie Zim giggled. Everyone knew about Mother's cooking trials.

"Expect about everyone to show up. Can't run out of food for Nick's last-night celebration, can we?" Auntie Zim said.

Nick was almost gone. My eyes started drowning again. "We already had a zillion people over here on Thursday," I grumbled. "And we cooked two whole days for the Fourth of July days."

"Get used to it, hon. Family—food. Friends—food. Good, bad, or whatever—it always means food," Auntie Zim said.

As soon as I hung up, something hit my back. I turned and saw Nick and Mother sitting at the kitchen table wearing silly grins. A small bundle of pale yellow art paper tied with a camouflage shoestring lay by my feet.

"Nice wrapping," I said, raising an eyebrow.

"Nothing but the best…" Nick said.

I sat down beside him and peeked at Mother. She smiled. I felt a little better. I untied the shoestring and slipped my finger under the taped creases. Inside was a folded scarf. I lifted it by its delicate rounded edging and flicked it open. I'd never seen anything so beautiful. Ever.

The background was shades of peacock blue—my favorite color. A bright gold and black cheetah lay in the middle. I supposed it was female because another cheetah stood with its nose pressed to hers. A heart frame packed with butterflies, exotic birds, and tropical flowers in pink, orange, and white surrounded them. I wanted to dive inside their fantasy world.

"Check this out, Little Dove—or should I say *squirt?*" Nick said.

"What?" I answered, not wanting to leave my dreamy haze.

"That scarf in your hands is a genuine, authentic…" Nick's voice trailed off. I waited, watching him. Maybe I was catching Birdie's lack-of patience disease because a few seconds later, impatience crawled up my spine like a scratchy caterpillar.

"Can you please finish your sentence?"

"Huh? Oh sure," he said, pretending he forgot what he was doing. "It's an absolute…one and only…"

Mother and I weren't breathing as we curved toward him.

"Hermes of Paris scarf," he said, leaning back in his chair like a good king giving away part of his kingdom.

Mother and I exchanged quick looks. I dropped my eyes to the scarf. What was Nick talking about?

He laughed and slapped his hand on his camo pants. "I never heard of Hermes scarves either until my bud's girlfriend dumped him. See…" Nick U-turned out of his chair and crouched energetically on the floor. Mother and I prepared for a lively Nick Story. "…my friend Clive buys this one in LA to give to his girlfriend as a gift when he proposes to her. Which he intended to do on his next leave, like two weeks away. Three days before his leave, he gets a letter from this chick and she's backing out. She's gonna marry her old boyfriend—the one with his neck tattooed in snakes! Man, Clive is torked! He grabs a fancy box out of his locker and rips the gold paper on it to shreds. That's when I get my first look at the scarf. He runs to the toilet to flush it, screaming like it's a real person—'I don't care if you cost $360, you're going down!'" Nick choked an invisible neck.

Mother cupped her hand over her mouth.

"I'm thinking his girlfriend did Clive a big favor, and he should just forget her and her loser boyfriend. But he's in bad shape. I step in and help him out. I offer him two of my ink sketches for the scarf. I tell him he can flush, rip, or stomp them. Whatever he wants. By now, he's not as mad. He says if I give him my watercolor—*Warrior Horse*—it's a deal." Nick pivoted back into his chair.

"Now *my* sister gets to wear the baddest scarf on the Rez," Nick said, winking at me.

I was so far on the edge of my seat, a butterfly sneeze would have put me on the floor. What a story! My blue mood turned into kettle steam and rose to the ceiling.

Grandmother rapped once on the kitchen door and stepped inside. She glared at the three of us, then zeroed in on me. I gulped. "Come sit while I weave in the morning. Not too late."

Her special invitation astonished me. Her eyes were blistery red, but she didn't seem angry. "Is six okay?" I was trying to be extra nice.

"Eight is better." She left. I wondered why she'd changed the time to later. Usually, the earlier the better with my grandparents.

Mother flashed me an odd look. She pushed her chair under the kitchen table and headed down the hall with a mysterious smile. "There it is," she said. "The balance. Everything unfolding as it should."

What in Sheep-Shears heck was she talking about?

"Must be a girl thing," Nick said, pulling his Phoenix Suns cap low on his head. "Hey, kid. Before I help Grandfather unload fertilizer, I have some advice for you."

"What? And I'm not a kid."

"Algae and expensive silk…" Nick shook his head and furrowed his brow. "…not a good combo. I don't think I'd dip that Hermes scarf in any horse troughs for at least…" he bit his lip, "…oh, a week or two."

He dodged the crumpled piece of art paper I tossed at his head.

"Oh, please don't hurt me," he begged, backing out the kitchen door.

I pounced on the phone like a *mosí* on a night moth and pressed in Birdie's number. Manny answered. Birdie wouldn't be home until late tonight.

It was time to be Nick's shadow for the rest of today. And in the morning, maybe I'd get answers to at least some of my questions.

Chapter 25

Two Girls From Two Grey Hills

NDER THE ARBOR, Grandmother sat ax-handle straight on the pine bench in front of her tabletop loom. A brown, white, and blue weaving was being born inside the strings—a piece of Grandmother's heart to send with her youngest daughter, Zim, to Albuquerque.

Her eyes followed me as I walked toward her. She took a sip from a fat white coffee mug and set it back on the table. A light wind blew steam off the top of a pot hanging above the fire pit. I smelled heated, uncooked beans, chili powder, onions, and oil. An oily-bottomed iron skillet and a stirring stick were on a flat rock beside the pit. I didn't know what to expect. I eased down on Grandfather's straw-bottomed chair like a shy feather. The delicious scent of fresh fry bread seeped from underneath a towel. Next to it was a jar of honey and a spoon.

Grandmother threaded a piece of blue yarn horizontally through the warp and combed it into the top of the weaving. "Eat," she said, not looking up.

I did.

"Listen…and I will tell you a story about life."

Two Girls from Two Grey Hills
(as told by Grandmother)

In Two Grey Hills once, two girls were like sisters. Shared lives. Laughed and cried together. Many hard times back then. Came a day, the families said the two girls have to go to the Indian boarding school down in Phoenix. Girls beg. They don't want to go.

First Girl's mother said, "No, she can't go." First Girl's father said, "Yes. She needs education. She goes." Same thing with Second Girl.

Anglo school wasn't happy. Girls cried so many tears there. Not allowed to speak their Diné language. Can't honor the People's old traditions. Teachers cut their long hair off and made them wear Bilagaana *clothes. Made them feel ashamed.*

Years passed. Slow. Then, something else happened. First Girl's mother, she got sick—sick bad. Lung sickness took her away. First Girl had to come home to live. She was thirteen years old by then. She took care of the family. Did the cooking. Took care of sheep, but not the big herds like they had before the government took so many away. Lots of work. She fixed mutton. Beans. Made good bread. Grew corn too. Sheared the sheep and spun yarn. Washed clothes. Gathered plants and roots for dyeing wool. Everything.

Second Girl had to stay at boarding school without First Girl. She is so sad without her. She cries and cries. First Girl cries all the time too. Second Girl finished that Indian school and went to a high school. Girls get to be together again in summers. Better times now. Girls still sister-friends. Forever, they promised.

One time, they made a special rug together. The girls don't care how long it takes. They do it anyway. Everyone in the village says it's the best rug on the Reservation. The most beautiful. The girls were very proud. They begin another rug like the first one so they will both have a rug from each other's hands. Good thing to do that.

One summertime, First Girl is sixteen, and Second Girl is fifteen. Kin of a good neighbor comes to the village, a cousin. A Marine home from war. Both girls invited to a big celebration like we have for Nick tonight. A loco thing happened. Both girls go crazy and want this soldier for a husband. They get so jealous. Say terrible things to each other. Bad, bad medicine. Now, they are not friends anymore. Both girls want the soldier, but he only wants First Girl.

Marine soldier talks with First Girl's father. Father says okay, you can get married when war is done. First, you help grow up First Girl's brother and sisters. Soldier only laughed. He told the First Girl's father he wants many children. Good to start with First Girl's family.

Marine leaves back to war. He gives First Girl a special picture of him. She loved it so much, she took it everywhere like it was a real person. It went to the sheep pastures. To hills to gather pinion nuts. When she cooked, she put it on a rock and spoke to it. Not just a picture to her. No.

Summer came again. Second Girl comes back to the village. Oh, very terrible. If both girls were on the same road, they turned their backs to each other. People tried to help, but no good. Their friendship is broken. Girls never talked together again. Not ever.

War got finished when First Girl was seventeen. For one year, her and her Marine *wrote letters together in pretty good English. One day, new soldier comes to Two Grey Hills. Younger. He is first soldier's good friend. He carries sad news on his back. First Girl's soldier won't come back to marry her. No, he won't come back. Korean War has swallowed him up forever.*

Grandmother rocked back and forth holding her head. I'd never seen her like that. She looked up at me through damp eyes.

"Silki, I am First Girl. Anna Yazzee is Second Girl."

Huh? Anna Yazzee and my grandmother best friends? Enemies? They made the rug Mrs. Anna carries with her all the time? They loved the same man?

"Marine's name, Ted Lee. Almost my husband. Good man. Marine's friend, Preston Benally. Good man too." Grandmother folded her hands on the tabletop.

"My Grandfather Preston?" I managed to squeak.

Grandmother nodded. She stared at the past through faraway eyes. "When we came to this place, I buried for good my picture of Ted Lee. Found a special place where the Concho Twins join hands. All this time, my picture was safe in the tree that becomes two trees. Special place? No! Not special. Ted Lee comes back to mock two bitter hearts. Me not forgiving Anna. Anna not forgiving me. Not good for nothing! Too many years lost like sand in the wind." Grandmother's face crumpled.

She had never let me see her cry. I hated it.

"Listen to my words, daughter. Hearts not forgiving turn dark." Grandmother swayed with her eyes closed. A few minutes passed. I wasn't sure I was breathing, but I knew I was shivering. Grandmother opened her eyes.

"Dark hearts turn bitter and trap you like prison bars. Make you so lonely…like a prisoner. Steal your *hozho*. That's how I lived…too many years."

Tired relief smoldered from Grandmother's moist eyes. Her eyes were powerful tools. Right now, they were beautiful.

As if by secret signal, Birdie's Nalí Anna materialized from the side of the brush arbor. She ignored us and walked over to the pot of beans. She leaned forward to sniff and picked up the stirring stick. "Sarah, these beans smell too spicy. Are you trying to burn holes in our bellies so we can't eat too much?" To me, her words sounded rude. I glanced at Grandmother. I couldn't believe it—she wore the hugest smile.

My mind started twirling like a baton at a Tseyi High School parade. Memories and questions spun in my head—like the look that came into Mrs. Anna's eyes whenever she asked about my family. Her stares when she thought I wasn't looking. The way she made me wait outside Birdie's gate in the hot sun a few weeks ago, even pretending she didn't see me! Was she getting even with Grandmother when she did that?

When did Mrs. Anna and Grandmother make peace? Did our parents help? Why didn't Mrs. Anna bring Birdie to hear Grandmother tell their story?

Mrs. Anna rustled past me smelling like fresh rain. She stopped in front of Grandmother, turned her head and winked at me. I heard a fly buzzing far away and realized it was walking on my arm. My eyes burned from forgetting to blink.

"You have not suffered alone, my sister," Mrs. Anna said, slightly louder than a whisper. She gathered her rose-colored crinkle skirt to the side and delicately slid down the bench on the opposite side of the table from Grandmother. The end of her silver Concha belt clinked on the wood as she moved.

She said something I couldn't hear. Grandmother answered her in the same low tone and pushed her loom aside. At first, they spoke to one another in English peppered with Navajo words. Slowly, they switched to *Diné Bizaad*, their heart language of fifty-six years ago. Years melted off their faces as they talked, gestured and finally...laughed.

I watched in silent awe, as if I were seeing a bashful stream swell into a mighty river. Invisible, I rose from the chair and walked the short path to my house in deep thought. My life was different now, and I knew it. I had shared in something before and beyond my years. For the first time, I could see my grandmother and Mrs. Anna as young women—not much different from Birdie and me.

But how did *Wol-la-chee* find Grandmother's picture in that mixed-up tree? Why would He leave it on Birdie's porch swing? Why did He take Birdie's ball?

My head churned with so much *how-why-why* inside it. Only one thing would help—downloading it all into Birdie's head.

Chapter 26
Friends and Foes

BEFORE I FINISHED PUNCHING in Birdie's number, the phone rang in my hand.

"Hello?"

"*Ya'at'eeh*, Silki. Did you get my postcard?" Birdie's voice coming through the telephone felt like ointment to my slashed heart. She had cut it to shreds that awful morning at the corral. Her postcard to me had helped, but it wasn't enough to heal all my wounds. I struggled not to cry. That would be so babyish.

"Silki?"

"Yeah…I got your card."

"Okay." Birdie said. "I missed the Fourth of July days. First time, huh?"

"Uh-huh."

"Um, you might not recognize me."

"That's for sure," I couldn't help saying.

"No…I mean, guess what? *Nali* and my dad surprised me with an early birthday present. I have contacts. No more glasses sliding down my nose."

Now that was news, and she was sharing it with me. My heart started healing fast.

"Clear or colored contacts?" I asked.

"Just clear. But Mom said if I take good care of them, I might get tinted ones for Christmas."

"Oh-my-gosh. Can you see yourself with violet eyes, Birdie?" I fell back onto the floor and scissored my legs in the air. "Have you seen Tito since the fire?"

"Tito's totally fine, even his leg. Mr. Tso called Dad and told him all about it while I was gone. Hey, you rock getting him out of the shed and everything. Thanks, Silk."

"Tito is my family too—you know that," I said, my smile threatening to crack my face. "Hey, why not spend the night with me after Nick's party? We have tons of stuff to catch up on. Can you believe our grandmothers kept the whole legend of their lives such a giant secret?"

"What giant secret?"

"You don't know about it yet? Get ready, Birdie. You're gonna howl at the moon when I tell you! Hey, just come over right now so we can get started."

"Well, you know, I really wanted to go to Nick's party, Silki, but…"

Birdie's words felt like a bowling ball hitting me in the nose. In a quadrillion years, I wouldn't have believed she would miss saying good-bye to Nick. Especially since she'd been gone his whole leave time. All her family, and most of the town, would be at the celebration tonight.

I couldn't talk. Birdie could.

"I promised Ronnie, um…she's this girl I met at camp. Anyway, I told her I'd spend a few days with her when I got back from my *Nalí's*. She's splitting for Utah in a few days. She spends the summer with her grandparents. She loves them, but it's really isolated where she goes. Not even a town. No grocery store or anything. She doesn't have many friends, and I was, you know, sorry for her."

I was sorry for me. I held the phone away from me, but Birdie's voice still came through it to torture me more.

"Ronnie and her mom are driving over from Fort Defiance to get me pretty soon. Can you tell Nick bye for me? Anyway, he's coming back in August for a lot longer, right?"

I had to grit my teeth to keep from screaming at Birdie. I didn't want her even saying my brother's name. I forced myself to sound happy—she didn't deserve to share my real feelings anymore. My heart was hard, but I laughed softly.

"Sure, I'll tell Nick for you. The party isn't such a big deal anyway. Probably boring. Oh, Grandmother needs me for something. See you, Birdie." I dropped the phone back in the charger breathing like I'd marathoned across the whole Navajo Nation. I climbed into Father's overstuffed chair and buried my face in scarves.

Now I understood how two girls could be the best friends in the world and then, just like that, hate each other's guts. How they could stop speaking to one another for fifty-six years like Grandmother and Mrs. Anna did. Right now, fifty-six years seemed too soon to speak to my former best friend.

Grandmother warned me about letting bitterness trap me. Would I let my bad feelings turn my heart dark and make me a prisoner? I could almost hear the metal bars locking into place.

Chapter 27
The Earring

ICK'S FRIEND CURTIS reminded me of a Brahma bull. I couldn't help smiling when he oozed out of his vintage VW Beetle in front of our house right after sunup. We were all sitting on the porch waiting for him. Everyone except Grandmother. She said her good-bye to Nick last night after the party, holding his hands and speaking to him in a low voice. Nick listened, nodded, then scooped her off her feet and swirled her around. We held our breaths. Grandmother scolded him in between laughs. Nick got away with things no one else dared.

Last night, Birdie's meanness, Grandmother's secret life, and Nick's leaving for the Marine base in Twenty-Nine Palms, California, stumbled around in my head like three sheep on locoweed. I wiggled up one side of my bed and down the other. Sometimes I punched my pillow and yelled at *Wol-la-chee*. Because of Him, Smiles and I couldn't escape to Red Rocks or Concho Mountain to forget our troubles anymore.

Crying into my hands, I swore Nick would wave good-bye to my best happy face the next morning, and that I didn't need a best friend anyway, and that I would find a way to rid my life of the Ancient Ant Man.

Later, I flipped through the scarf-tying book Auntie Zim gave me last Christmas and practiced tying my Hermes scarf into a French-Twist knot. Wearing it solo was the highest honor I could give any scarf.

Too soon, we stood in our doorway making sure the corners of our mouths pointed up, not down. Nick and Curtis took off for Albuquerque in the squatty car. I imagined Curtis' feet moving underneath the Beetle like in the old Fred Flintstone cartoons. The car rolled a few yards and stopped. Nick long-legged it back to us.

"Forgot to keep a promise," he explained, leaning toward my ear.

"The design on Geri's fingernail is from something she remembers her father wearing, like a medallion or something. She doodles it when she's talking. She's pretty closed up about her family. That's all I found out this time. Except we're definitely not from the same clans. Cool, huh?"

Nick pressed his thumb to mine, grinned all around, and was gone.

I'd forgotten about asking him to check Geri's fingernail for me. I didn't even care right now. Compared to Nick going away, it seemed like nothing.

The rest of the morning was slower than cold honey. How could I concentrate on diphthongs and consonants?

None of the high and rising tonal marks of our language made any sense today. I leaned into the computer screen and wished it would swallow me up. I felt one hundred percent grouchy about everything.

I barely spoke to Geri when we exchanged the ladybug. I knew she wanted to say something about my scarf. Who could blame her? It was gorgeous. Today, it belonged only to Nick and me.

Mother and I were climbing into the truck after classes when Auntie Jane's dandelion yellow pickup pulled into the parking lot, rotated in a tight half-turn, and stopped beside us. The driver's door opened a few inches. Coral toenails in white leather sandals dropped to the pavement. Legs in white jeans followed. The door pushed open, and there stood Auntie Jane with a turquoise and white polka dotted shirt and round white earrings the size of shooter marbles on her ear lobes.

"Hi, I'm glad I caught you two. I have a question for Silki." She walked toward me with an outstretched hand. "Look at this, hon. Do you recognize it?"

"It's my earring," I said.

"Ah-ha! I knew it. I wouldn't forget the earrings I bought my own niece for her birthday, would I? Didn't you say you lost one on Concho Mountain?

"Uh, yes."

Last summer, Birdie and I sort of disobeyed and went a little nuts one boring afternoon. We followed Mustang Canyon over to Toho Rock, a two-story sloped rock on the east side of Concho Mountain's Twin II. We weren't allowed over there, and we knew it. We wanted to find out why Nick and his friends always went on Saturday afternoons. We found out why.

Toho Rock's natural funnels in the rock surface, and the thick layers of soft sand above and below it, made it a perfect natural slide. It turned Birdie and me into craziacs for hours. When Birdie noticed one of my earrings missing, we searched for it but couldn't find it.

Afterward, we felt guilty for violating our parents' trust. We swore we'd never do it again. I mentioned I lost my earring on Concho Mountain but left out the "where" part.

I took the turquoise-tipped feather earring from Auntie Jane. The silver had tarnished to almost black. "Thanks, Auntie. Um…how'd you find it?"

"That's what's so crazy. It found me. Today is my day of the month to collect cans and greens for the Relief Center. I got my usual too-early-to-live start because of the fruit and veggies in this heat," Auntie Jane said.

Mother fidgeted beside me. "Let's get in the truck and finish this," she said. "I'll turn on the air."

It *was* hot, but I knew Mother was antsy to drive me home so she could bury herself in her books at the college library all afternoon. Then she wouldn't think so much about Nick. We climbed in the truck, me in the backseat. Auntie Jane started back in as soon as the doors closed.

"Well, as you know, I take everything to the Center for sorting and re-boxing before it goes out on the Rez about nine. Today I had seven plastic bags of cans and boxes and nine bags of produce. I worry about some of those folks opening their canned goods, so I pitched in and bought ten little cheap can openers."

Mother squirmed up front.

"I drank lots of coffee this morning, so I was feeling the call of nature, if you know what I mean. It was only a little after eight, so I drove by the house. That way I could let ChaCha out a few minutes and freshen up." Auntie Jane freshened up on the hour. She freshened up her rescue dog, ChaCha, nearly as often.

"Zim called, so I guess I was inside the house about ten minutes. Before I drove off, I happened to glance in the back of my truck. Can you believe those can openers were all lined up in a row like little tin soldiers? Silki's earring was right along with them, straight in a line. I took a count. Two sacks of cans, a bag of green stuff, and two can openers were just…gone!" She let out an exasperated sigh and looked from Mother to me.

My insides shriveled like a picked turnip drying in the sun. *Wol-la-chee* never gave it a rest, did He?

"Are you sure you counted right?" Mother said.

"Oh, sure. I'm careful about my tallies. I record them in a little spiral book in my glove box. No mistake. But what in Sheep's Wool was Silki's earring doing back there with the can openers? I'm sorry, but I feel like someone's playing a mean little joke on me." Auntie Jane's chocolaty eyes looked hurt. Her frown made her constant dimples disappear.

Mother donned a phony concerned look, shook her head, and shrugged her shoulders. She didn't intend to put much thought into solving Auntie Jane's mystery when she was suffering over her son. In the rearview mirror, she shot me a we're-out-of-here look. "Only time will tell, I suppose," she tsk-ed. I didn't think her words fit Auntie Jane's problem at all.

Auntie Jane pulled the handle and pushed the door open a few inches. She turned to look at me. "You want up here, babe?" she asked. I shook my head. "Well, let me know if you hear any buzz about this. If someone needed food, that's fine. Sure it is. I just don't understand why that little earring…" her voice faded away. She got out and leaned back inside.

"Okay, you two. See you Sunday at Mom's for lunch. And Jeanette…Nick's coming back in August." She smiled a sister smile at Mother. Mother looked a little embarrassed but returned the smile.

Auntie Jane reached through the divided seats and stroked my Hermes scarf. "Mm Mm, that Nick sure has good taste." She backed out and closed the door.

Mother saluted her, put our truck in gear and wasted no time rolling us onto the highway. I burrowed into the backseat and let the air conditioning vent frost my face. Now it matched my icy heart.

Part III

Chapter 28
Face Your Enemies

SPECIAL FORCES COMBAT soldiers smear real blackout on their faces and arms before battle. I didn't have any. What I did have was a major fed-up attitude.

I stared in the mirror. I saw a warrior in a black U.S. Marines Corps cap over pinned-up hair. She wore black jeans, black T-shirt, and purple hiking boots. The boots kind of ruined it, but I ignored that.

"Who are you anyway?" I asked myself.

I am Diné, a proud and brave person of history.

I raised a fist in the air. "Oo-rah!" I ground out with as much Marine spirit as I dared with Father in the next room. I sighed. My life this summer made about as much sense as Smiles taking guitar lessons. In my eyes, *Wol-la-chee* had crossed the line.

My apologies and giving relics back to the Kingdom of the Ants hadn't stopped Him. Nick said desperate times called for desperate actions. Well, I was desperate for my old life back. Without fear. Without worry. Without Birdie. The Birdie part made my stomach hurt, but I'd get over it. That other girl wasn't *my Birdie* anymore.

D-Day was supposed to have been the day after the earring incident, but it didn't work out. That's because Auntie Zim left her bookkeeping classes early and came home with me to help Grandmother dye yarn. Jesse was cranky, and Grandmother made me ride stick horses with him. Smiles was so embarrassed, he sneaked out the back corral gate.

Auntie Zim and Jesse finally left, but two of Father's cousins dropped by unexpectedly on their way to Tucson. That meant a big supper and having to hang around to smile. They left the next day after wasting half of my Friday. I started into my room to change clothes for the Mission, but Grandmother herded me back to the kitchen to wash the dishes left crusting in the sink. She told me to sweep off our front porch after that.

Sheep Shears! How could anyone be a warrior in a family like mine?

I worked in an angry huff, sweeping the sand on the porch into my own *Desert Storm*. I was mad at my chores, mad at my family, and mad at *Wol-la-chee*. What if He refused to leave? Well, then…there would be trouble.

"Bring it on, buddy!" I shouted at the air, holding my broom like a sword. My *sword* was too heavy on the straw end, and it bumped to the concrete. I didn't let that bother me. Too much.

I named the Mission *Operation: Back Off!* because that's how I felt about everything. I was ready to rip Birdie's room apart to find the rest of her relics. With her out of town, Manny would let me inside to plunder.

One foot out of my room, I remembered my scarves lying on the bed. Did Marines wear scarves? I knew they were always prepared for battle and carried the proper military equipment. Weren't Smiles and my scarves the proper gear for me? Hmm. While I chewed my lip and thought about it, the phone rang.

"Silki, it's Birdie," Father called.

So Birdie was back from Fort Defiance. Now I'd have to ignore how much I was never going to speak to her again. I grabbed my scarf chain and headed down the hall. I smiled at Father as he handed me the phone and went out the kitchen door.

"Hey-I'll-be-over-to-look-for-your-missing-anthill-stuff-in-fifteen-minutes-I-know-some-of-your-hiding-places-better-than-you-do-and-I'm-coming-right-now-and-you-don't-need-to-help-me," I said as fast as I could.

Birdie giggled. "Practicing to be an auctioneer, Silk?"

I didn't answer. A few seconds later, Birdie cleared her throat. "Um, sure. I'll be home. Mom and Dad are at work. I guess Manny's over at his friend's house. Come over for the afternoon. We can—"

Our phone was back in its charger before Birdie finished her sentence. Hanging up on someone was another *first* for me. It felt mean and good at the same time.

Staying mega mad was important for Mission success. On the way to Birdie's, I talked to Smiles about how many ways the Ant Man had ruined my life this summer. That worked me up. Smiles snorted at all the right times. I pressed my heels about a quarter of an inch into his ribs, and he broke into a run. His speed matched my wild mood.

I marched up Birdie's path like a general on important duty, which, of course, I was. She was watching for me because the screen door opened like an automatic door at the Albuquerque Coronado Mall. Birdie's face wore a full-sized question mark.

"Okay if I start?" I pushed through the door without waiting for an answer.

"Silki?" Birdie asked when I had taken a few steps.

I stopped but didn't turn. "What?"

"Why are you dressed like that?"

"As Nick says, 'The element of surprise can tip the odds in your favor.'"

"Tip the odds?"

I sighed noisily. "I don't have time for gibberish, Birdie. I'll find your stuff *for you* and be out of here before you can blink. That all right with you?"

"Sure," she said in a voice as soft as a bug's whisper.

I wasted no time looting all the secret places in her room. Sprawled on my stomach, I dropped my fingers into the loose baseboard behind her bed. I felt something. I pulled out a tiny plastic bag with three bead fragments sealed inside. I dragged her chair under the overhead light and ran my hand over the flat glass fixture. Two tiny pieces of black pottery. I attacked the closet next.

"Silki?" Birdie's voice sounded far away, like I had cotton balls stuffed in my ears. I threw everything from one side of her closet to the other. I found her pink and green Celebration Circle dance bag like the one in my own closet. My hands shook as I unzipped the inside pocket and flipped open the metal mint box. Nothing.

I dove for her pencil cup on the card table and dumped it, poking through the mess. I found a tip of a red and grey flint arrowhead and a chip from an ancient grinding rock.

"There's nowhere else to look, girl," Birdie said. I shoved the pieces inside my pocket on top of a folded scarf holding the other pieces Birdie brought me after my trip to the anthill. I never wanted to see any of it again—not even my garnet.

I rotated on my heel and pulled my cap low on my forehead. "See you."

"Where are you going?"

"The mountain."

"Aren't you afraid of *Wol-la-chee* anymore?"

"Don't dare mock me, Birdie," I warned. Our eyes met. "Someone has to do it—it might as well be me. He has to stop stealing and…oh, forget it. You have no clue what's been happening around this Rez. You don't even know about our grandmothers and that Marine in the old photograph you found, do you?"

Her blown-away expression almost made me laugh.

"Yeah, that's what I figured. Guess they thought you were too young to know."

I whisked past her and out the door. She was outside standing by me so quick, it startled me. "Silki, I...just let me go with you. Please? I have to change my blouse so Mom won't get mad, but I can hurry."

What was this? Birdie acting nice and like she had time for me now?

"Hey, who needs *your* help with anything?" Birdie looked like I'd slapped her.

"Besides, I'm climbing Twin I from the road side. You know, the steep, south side with loose rocks and that slippery ridge cap at the top?"

"Why go through all that to return our junk to the anthill?"

I rolled my eyes. "Not that you need to know, but I'm looking for a strange tree somewhere between Twin I and Twin II. I don't know any other way to find it. From there, I have to hike down the north side. You know what that means."

Birdie looked lost.

"It means I have to find a way down from the cliffs without breaking my neck so I can dump those stupid-cursed-idiotic relics back on that pile of gravel and ants. And is that all I have to do? No!" My voice sounded squeaky. "*Operation: Back Off!* isn't finished until I face-off with *Wol-la-chee*. So, get it? This Mission is too dangerous for a prissy little volleyball girl like you."

"Gah, Silki, you sound so different."

I belly-laughed and wondered why I did. Birdie's face changed. She had the same look in her eyes as when we found the kitten with a broken leg behind the school last year. She put a hand on my arm.

"Listen, I know I—"

"Save it." I stomped down the porch steps. I was flinging the front gate open when a dribble of reasonable thinking leaked into my brain. What about Smiles? The south side of Concho Mountain was impossible for any horse to climb, and I would never leave him tied alone by the road.

It was like Birdie became a mind reader. "Poor Smiles," she said. "There's no shade for him at the bottom of south Twin I. And would he be safe? Just think, he and DelaRosa could play by the covered pen this afternoon."

Oh-my-gosh. Birdie sounded normal again. I was almost impressed. She continued.

"If we ride double on Paul McCartney, we'll get there twice as fast as walking. When we finish, it's only a few minutes from the anthill to your house if we jog. I can pick up my bike tomorrow."

I squinted up at the sun. Darkness would roll over our valley about eight tonight. It would be dark on the mountain before then. Three hours of daylight should be plenty of time. Even though I was nearly as brave as Nick now, I didn't want anywhere near Concho Mountain at night.

Birdie knew she was winning me over because she started unbuttoning her sleeve cuffs. "What kind of tree are you trying to find?" she asked.

If I told her, would she smirk?

"An unusual one. It's where I'm challenging *Wol-la-chee* to come out and face me. He knows why." Making my grandmother cry by stealing her special photo from that tree was another reason I was *bá ntseeshdá*.

"So go ahead and make fun of me if you want to, Birdie, but you don't know how He's messed with me this summer. No one does." My voice quivered on the last part. I coughed and fiddled with Smiles' bridle.

"I want to go with you, Silk," Birdie said in a tone that almost made me cry. I hoped my frown and tapping foot signaled I was close to being permanently annoyed with her. Letting her back into my life was scary in so many ways. *Mad* always felt better than *hurt*.

Wol-la-chee is Birdie's problem too.

True. *Wol-la-chee* was ticked off at both of us. I caved. "I'll take Smiles to the pen. Hurry up—I don't have all day," I said, as gruffly as any wartime commander would.

"Back in a flash," Birdie said, ducking into the house.

I reviewed my route with Smiles as we walked to the pen so he wouldn't be too upset about staying at Birdie's.

"Remember all the thick fourwing saltbush growing like a beard around the bottom of south Twin II, beauty? Yeah. Me too. I can't break through all that shrubbery to look for the tree that becomes two trees—the saltbush would tear my skin off. My only choice is crossing over the three foothills and climbing the rest of Twin I, you know?" Smiles was quiet.

Before now, I hadn't considered *Dibé* Valley in between the second and third foothills. The abandoned sheep camp up there would be creepy. Having Birdie with me for that part would be pretty okay.

I dragged the blanket off Smiles and rubbed my hands over his damp back. I could tell he wasn't convinced yet. "What do you think the Ancient Ant Man will do when I order Him off the Rez?" He nudged my shoulder. "Try to understand, Smiles. I just can't take you today."

I hung his gear on a nail and rearranged his forelock. "Listen, when you see me again, I'll be wearing the smell of victory." Smiles was too polite to roll his eyes.

I checked the water level in DelaRosa's water tub and fastened the corral gate behind me. I blew Smiles a kiss. His expression asked how I could go on an adventure and leave him babysitting a goat. Tough question.

Birdie came out of her house in a navy blue T-shirt, a pair of her mother's black workout pants, tennis shoes, and a black *God Bless America* cap I'd never seen before. She straddled her bike and flicked the kickstand up with her heel.

"Ready?" she asked.

"As a bull in a rodeo chute."

Chapter 29
Foothills

LISTENING TO BIRDIE'S VOICE on the way to Concho Mountain, I decided riding bicycles on ruffled roads would be good exercise for opera singers. Birdie vibrated through small talk and questions while we bumpity-rumped over a thousand ruts. I wondered why she was so chatty. I didn't feel like talking, so I didn't.

When we bailed off so Birdie could hand-guide Paul McCartney over the deepest grooves, I bent the bill of my cap into a tighter U-shape and trotted beside her to keep our pace fast. When she looked like she had another question, I said, "Let's roll, Birdie."

Mentioning our grandmothers and the Marine in the photo earlier had her curiosity running wild. I figured she had a great chance to hear all about it the night of Nick's party. Now she could just suffer. I still wondered why I was the only granddaughter invited to hear the Legend of the Two Girls from Two Grey Hills.

Once during our bike ride, Birdie asked me what I thought *Wol-la-chee* had done. What *I thought* He had done? She was still accusing me of living in a make-believe world. I bounced behind her on the hard buddy seat clenching my teeth until my jaws hurt.

At last, Destination Zero—or whatever they say in war movies. It was hard to ignore the juniper perfume lacing the air and the sage thrashers having chirp-meetings all around us, but I did.

While Birdie searched for a spot to leave her bike, I studied south Twin I. The other side of that little hump of mountain had been our fantasy playground since the fifth grade. How could two sides of the same hill be so different? Come to think of it, Birdie and Twin I were a lot alike.

"Hey, I think I'll hide Paul McCartney, you know?" Birdie called. I did know. Someone with tired feet might come along and *borrow* it. She hid it behind a stack of rocks surrounded by sage and greasewood.

"Can you see it from the road?" Birdie asked.

"No."

"Look who's coming."

Mr. Nakai and his flatbed truck swayed toward us inside a globe of road powder.

"Pretend we're rock hunting or something," I said. "In case he gabs with Father or Grandfather this afternoon."

Mr. Nakai's truck eased off the road beside the spiny saltbush clumps at the bottom of Twin II. His form bobbed up and down behind the grimy front window.

"What the heck is he doing in there?" Birdie asked, just before his front door opened with a dull metal click. He waved a walking stick over his head as a greeting. He had a cardboard box tucked under his arm.

"Oh no," I groaned, watching him stroll slowly down a pale burgundy wash full of weedy plants. He picked something up, examined it, put it in the box. He was probably gathering snakeweed and purple bee plants for Mrs. Nakai. His red-checkered shirt and dusty jeans disappeared from sight.

We waited—not patiently. Before I could start spewing, Mr. Nakai reappeared with a rusty can on the end of his stick and a box full of vegetation. In a few minutes, his truck creaked back onto the road. Birdie and I waved as if we were at a parade and Mr. Nakai was the only entry. I hoped we didn't look guilty.

"He's a hoot," Birdie said.

"Now that we've wasted a zillion hours," I grumbled. I rotated my scarf chain to hang down my back and stepped toward the first foothill.

"Silki?"

"What?"

"You sure are mad at me."

I ignored her words and dashed up the first foothill like a rabbit in a 10K. I reached the top and trotted down the backside.

"Silki?" Birdie called behind me.

"Yeah?"

"What are you the most mad about?"

I snorted and started up the side of the second foothill in a run.

"Are you a race horse?" Birdie yelled at my back.

She was kidding with me. Part of me wanted to stop being annoyed, but her horse comment reminded me of Tito. I could never forgive her for giving him up.

I jogged until I felt lightheaded. Had I eaten today? Early, before Father and his cousins had their breakfast marathon. What about water? No, just a glass of apple juice before changing into my *Operation: Back Off!* clothes. Not very smart Marine behavior.

My black clothes were sucking up extra sunshine and making my T-shirt stick to my back. Now I got it why Auntie Jane said dark clothes weren't so hot for hot weather.

I slowed, breathing hard the rest of the way to the top. I plopped down on a rock close to a tiny, hectic anthill and fanned my face with my cap. The wind cooled my hot head. I noticed deer and fox tracks in the dirt by my boots.

Birdie topped the rise and squatted beside me. She smelled like watermelon gum. She looked awesome without glasses falling down her nose. I wanted to tell her, but the hard rock in my stomach said *no.*

"Wow. Nice up here," she said. "Let's ride our horses up the first two foothills and have a picnic sometime. I didn't see any deep holes or shale."

I jumped up hitting my cap against my leg. "Our horses? Where's yours, Birdie? Oh, yeah. At the neighbor's. Dumped, like an old junk car."

"Hey, will you chill? I couldn't leave Tito alone while I was at camp—"

"You sent him away because of volleyball? Oh yeah. That shouldn't surprise anyone." I backed away feeling a little like I hated Birdie.

"You know my parents don't have time to mess with him."

"Neither do you. Or anyone else." I shot off, straining to put distance between us.

"That's not so, Silki," Birdie called after me, her voice vanishing into the atmosphere.

Far away from me—that's how I wanted Miss Yazzee. Probably forever. Why did I ever let her come with me?

I worked my way down the side of the second foothill partly sliding on my rear and mumbling under my breath about Birdie. Not even looking, I veered sharply to the right at the bottom. A muffled, cushiony feeling under my boots made me look down. Thick grass grew higher than my ankles.

Dibé Valley.

The wind chanted lonesome melodies as it gusted across the high places watching over the little valley. I sank to my knees in the emerald meadow and stared at Lincoln Chee's tumbledown sheep camp. I'd never seen a sadder place.

Droopy cottonwood trees stooped like old guards over the structure. The roof slumped. A gap by the hinges of the boarded-up door facing east looked like a silent scream. That was scary. Rotting arbor posts in the front leaned tiredly toward the ground. The posts were topped by a weather-beaten hunk of lattice crusted with wads of dirty brush. A round, stone-stacked sheep pen near the hogan was starting to crumble.

Behind it, water trickled from a rocky niche in the side of the third foothill. It pooled into a spoon-shaped rock at the bottom. Natural water like that was unusual around here. No wonder Mr. Chee, Grandmother, and lots of other sheepherders brought their sheep to this place in the hot summer months. Nowadays, only a few people raised sheep around Mesa Redondo. For the last few years, Grandmother bought Churro sheep wool from the Black Mesa weavers.

Birdie huffed to a stop beside me. "Gah, Silki. That's where, uh, old Mr. Chee, you know…" The subject of death was mostly unmentionable among the *Diné*. Some folks never again spoke a departed's name.

"I know," I whispered. "Nick told me about it. Depressing, isn't it?"

"You don't think Mr. Chee's *chindi*…" Birdie's voice faded away. Mr. Chee had passed away inside his hogan. Except for removing his corpse through the north wall, no one had touched the little mud and log building since then. Some folks believed that the door coming loose meant Mr. Chee's *chindi* had escaped to haunt the living. That was kind of normal thinking on the Rez.

"Let's go." I led us along the edge of the valley. Our eyes were pasted to the old hogan like it might rise up and shout *Boo!* The slightest unnatural noise would have sent us into shriek fits. Behind me, Birdie hung onto my scarves. We pressed our hot palms to the cool water wall and sipped from our cupped hands. I splashed water on my face and double-dog wished I'd brought an Almond Joy or some pinion nuts with me.

We climbed the easy slant of the third foothill in silence, sidestepping hedgehog cactus and animal burrows. The foothill fastened onto the side of the mountain and had no downside. On top of its flat mesa, we were more than two-thirds up the south side of Twin I. The last third was bald except for scraggly sage, packed pinkish dirt, and slippery shale.

I wondered why Twin I and Twin II were called twins. They weren't alike in shape, height, or vegetation.

"Pretty tricky, Birdie," I said, gazing up at our slim climbing options. "We'll have to step onto that little ledge underneath the ridge and work our way around its curve. I can probably see into the gap from there. Then we'll slide down to the right spot." I stepped, and Birdie grabbed my arm.

"I have to tell you something," she said, talking fast. "Tito's coming home tomorrow. I've tried to tell you all day, but you weren't listening to me. I need him home. He's my baby."

"Tito? Coming home tomorrow?"

"Yes. I have so much to tell you, Silki, but as Dad always says, 'daylight's burning.'"

Just like that, a wheelbarrow full of *mad* dumped right out of me. I felt like doing a dance or something to celebrate, but Birdie was right. Darkness would soon pull its blanket over Concho Mountain.

Chapter 30

A Tree that Becomes
Two Trees

I T TOOK A FULL-BELLY WRAP to climb the rest of south
Twin I. Birdie stayed close as we made our way to the
stony ledge running parallel to the golden brow at the
top. It hadn't looked this steep from the road. No way
could I see Grandmother climbing like a mountain goat
to get to her tree. I wished I knew her shortcut.

"Still there?" I asked Birdie, keeping my eyes focused
ahead.

"Yeah, just a little...out of...breath. How far..." Birdie
sucked in a gob of air. "... do we walk along that ledge
thing? It looks so narrow."

"Until I spot the special tree.

"What's it look like?"

"Like one tree that starts looking like two trees."

I eased my foot onto the ledge before adding my
weight. It felt rock-solid but almost too shallow for my
clunky hiking boots. I stepped onto it grabbing rocky

tentacles, deformed twigs, and ropey weeds—anything to stop gravity from yanking me down the sharp sides. Birdie was a good climber too, but this was hard. It was taking up too much time too.

I started worrying. We'd have to complete the rest of *Operation: Back Off!* in express mode. And what if *Wol-la-chee* wasn't on Concho Mountain today? I couldn't actually have a face-off without Him, could I? What if someone driving on the road spotted us hugging the side of the mountain like spider monkeys? They might think we were in trouble and stop to help. Or, worse, call our parents.

The wind started settling down. That meant evening was pressing in on us. When we rounded the cap rock, it started looking like *our* Concho Mountain below. I wiped my eyes on my sleeve and spied a patch of green below. Two treetops were taller than the rest.

"Hey, Birdie, ready to ditch this moon crater? I think I see the tree. Guess we can slide down on our stomachs."

"Where is it…uh, uh…Silki, help me!" Birdie dropped away from me in a dusty avalanche of powder and pebbles. Her desperate fingers resembled lizard toes as she clawed at the loose dirt.

She screamed.

I screamed as her frightened face disappeared beneath the slant of the hill.

"Birdie!"

This is all your fault, a fly-by pinion jay scolded.

"Hush!" I hissed at him. A soft updraft cooled my face. I realized my cheeks were covered in tears. What if *Wol-la-chee* got Birdie?

"I'm coming, Birdie!"

I pressed my body against the hard dirt and baby-hopped off the ledge. I forgot to arch. Sharp edges scraped along my torso. I groaned all the way to the bottom.

A mound of rabbitbrush cradled me like a beach ball, tickling my face with its leaves. Totally disgusted, I rolled onto ground that was more rock than dirt. It took a few minutes to untangle my shirt from the bush.

I called Birdie through cupped hands, then rescued my cap from its upside-down landing. I pulled the rest of the hairpins out of my messy hair. My stomach skin burned like fire, but that was beside the point when I looked behind me.

What in Sheep-Shear heaven was this unbelievable place...a miniature version of *Tse'bighanilini*—Upper Antelope Canyon? When our family visited that canyon in Page, Arizona, I couldn't talk for two hours after we left. Now, here was a scaled-down version of a slot canyon right here on Concho Mountain. My family was brilliant for not telling me about it.

Peach-colored rocks plumped and rolled in striated swirls. They looked like pulled taffy turned into petrified stone by a nature magician. They invited me to step inside their narrow halls.

Did I hear a soft voice calling, or was it wind shearing around the rocks? I wiped dirt off my lips with the bottom of my T-shirt. My concentration was blurring. I blamed it mostly on the temptation of that slot canyon. I turned my back on it.

I climbed a few feet to a gateway made of pale red stone. I ducked under its natural archway and walked down a hollowed-out rock channel. The green area I'd seen from the top of south Twin I unfolded in front of me.

Cedars spread their round skirts on the ground. Junipers rose in wrinkly alien shapes toward the sky. Scrubby oak leaves wiggled like little bells in the evening wisps. Pines whispered ancient stories to one another. That's when the weakness started. I was suffering from too-much-scenery shock.

Pay no attention to this conspiracy of nature. Find Birdie.

Right. Birdie. Christmas greenery scents teased my nose while I walked through the wooded maze calling her in a low voice.

"Over here."

Whew. Birdie was safe. I wound through the trees and found her straddling an earth gash about a foot wide. I knew it had to be the erosion line that turned into Mustang Canyon below the cliffs. Birdie looked like she'd showered in chalk dust and puffed her face with pale powder. But her bright smile looked like the old days.

"Look, Silk," she said reverently, pointing with her cap at the juniper tree standing in front of her. A gnarly trunk grew about eight feet before it coiled into a wooden knot. Two branches growing from the bulge angled into a perfect "Y." *A tree that becomes two trees.*

I circled it, staring up at the two tree arms praising the sky. Charcoal-colored rocks with lava dimples sat like listeners around the trunk—probably Grandmother's stepping-stones for burying Mr. Ted Lee's picture in the tree's wrinkle.

"Okay, what's up with this tree?" Birdie asked. "Besides that it's awesome."

"Why didn't you wait for me at the bottom of Twin I?" I asked.

"I don't know. I got a little hypnotized with those crazy rocks and everything. I started climbing and wound up here."

I understood. The slot canyon had almost put me in a coma.

"You look all right after your fall," I said.

"Hey—you keep changing the subject. Aren't you going to tell me about this tree, or anything else I've asked you today?"

"Hang on. I told you when I stood in front of this tree, I was ready to face the Ancient. That's the Mission, Birdie. Don't get sidetracked." I took off my cap and backed up against the tree. "So, if He's here...He can come out and face me." I shivered. It was a good thing I was brave like Nick, or I would have taken off running. I waited at least four or five seconds.

"Well, okay then. We can't wait around here forever. Those ants need their relics back."

Birdie started to stay something.

"Later, Birdie. We'd better rock and roll." I was ready to move on. Fast.

Birdie hadn't made fun of me speaking to *Wol-la-chee*, and her eyes were huge when I tossed out my challenge to Him.

Did she finally believe?

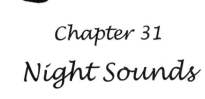

Chapter 31
Night Sounds

OST OF THE SPACE between the twin mountains turned out to be a rock bed related to the fifteen-foot-high rock cliffs crowning Concho Mountain on the north side. Looking over the side of them, I felt like a doodlebug. I had seriously underestimated the unfriendly climbing conditions. I slumped down cross-legged. "I'm out of ideas, Birdie."

Birdie smiled. "I'm not. My cousin Mark who works at the hospital told me a secret way off these cliffs. Bet Nick knows it too. Come on."

I watched in amazement as Birdie used her hand like a pointer, lining it up in the direction of north. She moved it several degrees left in a pie shape and lowered it. We walked in that direction. She counted scrubby bushes.

"One. Two. Three. Four. Follow me," she said, slipping behind one and disappearing.

"Birdie?" I ran around the bush and saw a hole large enough for a human. Its bottom dropped away in spiral curves.

If Birdie could do it, so could I. I lowered myself into what turned out to be the world's coolest tube slide. Loose pebbles and gravity carried me downward, spitting me into an eroded runoff hole about the size of Curtis' VW bug. Beside it was Mustang Canyon, wider and deeper now, but still a small canyon.

Birdie looked proud.

"Oh-my-gosh! That was almost more fun than Toho Rock. Why didn't you tell me about this when I said I needed a way off the cliffs without breaking my neck?"

"Would you have listened?"

She had a point.

Afternoon currents bounced off us and roosted in the trees. Nature's sounds were tucking in for the night. An owl hooted close by. Grandmother would have said that was a bad sign.

"Did you hear that? Do we absolutely have to go to Toho Rock?" Birdie asked.

"Yeah we do. The canyon split-off isn't far from here though."

Before *Wol-la-chee* crashed into our world, the Mustang Canyon split-off marked the top boundary our parents gave us on north Twin I. Today, Birdie and I were breaking all their rules. How could it turn out good?

"We can be at Toho Rock a few minutes after we reach the split. I told you I'm here to face *Wol-la-chee*."

"Has anyone ever told you you're toto-loco?"

"Yeah. Me."

I couldn't blame Birdie for being grouchy about my commitment to *Operation: Back Off!* She hadn't gone through the Ancient's pranks. Or had the wind knocked out of her from a rude shove to the ground. Come to think of it, she had been a good sport all afternoon—a lot like my *old Birdie*. Not one mean or sarcastic comment. Besides, Tito was coming home!

But I still had to do something about that rock in my stomach.

"Listen, Birdie." I locked eyes with her. "I never stole your volleyball. It was in our corral that morning. I was as shocked to see it as you were. If you can't believe me about that, well..." I stopped talking and waited.

Birdie dropped her head. "I know you don't lie, Silki."

That's all I needed to stop being mad. In return, as commander of the Mission, it was my duty to get Birdie fired up again.

"Okay. *Operation: Back Off!* needs women like you. Let's hit it." I hopped into the canyon at the shallowest end and looked back at Birdie. She wasn't moving. Maybe she needed more fuel in her tank. "Hey, you don't know about the earring I lost up here last year, do you?" I asked, taking small steps forward in the sandy-bottomed ravine.

"Duh—I was with you when you lost it."

I chuckled. "No, not that. I mean how it traveled from Toho Rock to the back of Auntie Jane's pickup this past Wednesday."

"How did it do that?"

"Exactly. Now you're getting it."

I heard Birdie's loud sigh as I took off. All the way to my little toes, I longed to share with her about my weeks of misery. If we hurried, maybe that could happen tonight. Now that was worth working for.

We kept a good pace winding along the canyon bottom and hopping over brush and rocks all the way to the split. I slanted to the right. Going straight would have slicked us right off the mountain.

"Hey, Earth to Silki—we could be at the bottom of Red Rocks dumping our anthill stuff in just a few minutes," Birdie called.

"What's that?" I answered, not slowing down.

"Oh, Sheep Shears…" were the last words I heard. I looked up. The first stars had taken their evening seats. A bulky cloudbank covered the western part of the sky. With my head in the clouds, I stumbled over an exposed root. It didn't hurt, but biting my tongue did. I rubbed my finger across it. Blood.

My stomach growled mournfully right before Birdie said something behind me.

"What, Birdie?"

A frog duet croaked somewhere. Birdie trudged into sight. I sucked in my breath. The evening light on her chalky clothes and face made her look like a spirit coming at me. Another reminder of why we were on the mountain.

"Are you resting?" she asked.

"Huh? No, I fell. Your clothes sure are dusty. From your fall down the mountain, I mean. What did you just say to me?"

"When?"

"Before you asked me if I was resting."

"Nothing."

"Yes, you—oh never mind," I said.

Birdie frowned and stretched. "I'm so starved. We're in big trouble for staying out this late. I've never done it before."

"I know. Let's climb out of the canyon. I'm just going to the top of Toho Rock, Birdie, not to the bottom. If *Wol-la-chee* doesn't show, we're out of here. You can wait for me here if you want. Trust me, I won't be very long."

"Um, no thanks."

Squaring off with the Ancient Ant Man in the dark hadn't been part of the plan. I'd come this far, though, so I had to try. That's what generals did.

We used rocks and roots to pull ourselves up the canyon wall. My scraped stomach felt shrink-wrapped, and my tongue burned. I heard something and paused to listen. Birdie banged into my heel.

"Why are you—?"

"Shhh. Listen." A low murmur came from somewhere. Birdie pulled up even with me.

"Gah, it's totally night out here," she said in a regular voice.

"Be quiet," I whispered. We scurried up the rest of the slant and clung underneath the lip of the canyon like aphids on a leaf.

Voices rode the night air. We were not alone on Concho Mountain.

Chapter 32
Toho Rock

E TWISTED OUT OF THE CANYON and lay flat. "Who would be up here at night?" Birdie whispered. I struggled for a logical explanation.

"Probably overnight campers."

"Here?"

Right. Concho Mountain wasn't exactly a tourist spot. Who else...Ancients? *Wol-la-chee's* haven? Was the Mission about to be fulfilled? My heart pounded so hard I heard waves crashing inside my ears.

"We have to go see, Birdie. Don't talk, okay?"

"Okay," she breathed.

We hunkered down and inched forward. My nerves were as tight as a four-inch hair scrunchee wrapped three times around Smiles. Just before I snapped apart, the sounds evolved into two voices. *Human voices.*

Instead of relief, a beehive full of worries stung me all over. Were Birdie and I really slinking through the trees at night on Concho Mountain? Would our parents think we were at each other's houses right now? No. The unwritten law was that we let them know where we were *before* dark.

The stinging-est worry was whether *Wol-la-chee* was watching and waiting for just the right moment to pounce on us.

I stole a look from behind a pine tree. A carroty glow lit up the top part of Toho Rock. Sparks twirled into the night sky. For the first time, I smelled pinion and cedar wood burning. Words and smoke traveled upward in the thin, cool air. Birdie and I edged closer.

I put my knuckle down on sharp needles and stifled a cry. "Watch out for cactus," I murmured in Birdie's ear, guiding us around a big bunch of it. I wet my knuckle with my sore tongue. We crept to the crown of Toho Rock and peeked over the side.

Below, a man leaned against the rock wall with one of his legs bent and the other one straight. His straight leg had a ripped place in the jeans about mid-thigh. It looked like a huge ace bandage was underneath the ripped part. Near him, a fire sputtered on a mound of dirt and sticks. A rock pushed close to the orange-blue flames had a pan sitting on it. The man balanced a tall bottle on his leg. I saw another pair of legs and some folded hands just inside the fire-lit area.

It was stone silent except for the sizzling pop of sap exploding inside the burning logs. A few night wrens twittered about the strangers. I squeezed Birdie's arm twice.

It was our signal to lie as still as dirt. Three squeezes meant to back up—part of the Silent Code we invented in the fifth grade.

I decided the men were probably travelers spending the night at Toho Rock. Maybe they used to slide on it when they were young like Nick and his friends did. Canned bean aroma drifting upward smelled as good as steak. Watching the flames made me drowsy. It made sense to go straight home and bring the anthill relics back tomorrow. That is, if Birdie and I ever got to leave our houses again after our parents were through grounding us.

A second before I gave Birdie the three-squeeze signal, the man leaning against Toho Rock made a loud snuffing noise in his throat and spat. Birdie and I jumped.

"You're nothing," he snarled, turning the bottle up to his lips. "I should have left you to rot too." He emptied the bottle and threw it. It shattered, sending Birdie and me into full-body tremors.

"Get me something else to drink, boy." The other person didn't move. "You hear me, you worthless mule? I'm thirsty."

The other pair of legs receded into the darkness. In a few moments, a slender guy wearing a cap brought the man a tall bottle. "It's the last one. Can't we save it?" he asked, holding the bottle out to the man.

"You trying to boss me around, Shonnie boy?"

"Don't call me that, Indie. Please."

"Aw...the little punk don't like his name." Indie grabbed the bottle from Shonnie and twisted the cap off. He took a long drink. "Ahh...fire water good, right boy? Want some?" He held the bottle toward Shonnie, who faced him with his arms at his sides. Indie laughed—a harsh sound. "Get me some of them beans. Scald me this time, and you'll be sorry."

Shonnie disappeared. He came back with a spoon and a cup. He squatted, stirred the pan, and spooned beans into the cup. After he gave it to Indie, he returned to the inky dark. The white tips of two tennis shoes appeared in the circle of light. I couldn't help feeling sorry for him.

This was our chance to back off and take off. Toho Rock night visitors were none of our business. The liquor was even more reason to run. It was against the law to bring alcohol like that to the Navajo Nation.

I squeezed Birdie's arm three times. She squeezed back two times. Huh? I glanced at her. She looked hypnotized. She shook her head *no* without breaking her stare.

Indie threw the spoon into the dark and rolled the cup along the ground. He wiped his mouth on the back of his hand and grunted. "Better make sure I get lots of time tomorrow. This leg ain't so good yet. You better be real talkative too. I'd just as soon crack that loser's scull and drive the truck off myself," he said.

Birdie and I stiffened like we'd been spray starched.

"It's okay, Indie." Shonnie's voice poured out smooth as syrup. He scooted into the light. "I have it handled. You'll have plenty of time to get settled in the back end. That old guy's never in a hurry. I'll ask him to drop me off at the gas station. He'll leave, and we can go in and…and…"

Indie blew a hateful "Ha!" A few seconds later, he said, "You're a joke!" He swigged from the bottle. "Let me help you talk, mama's boy. Me and you are gonna rob—that's R-O-B—that Lobo Gas place of every d—n thing they got. I need cigarettes. Food. Something to drive, and…" Indie laughed a smoker's wheezy laugh. "…yeah, I might even get me a girlfriend."

Indie spit through his front teeth. It made an angry *phssst* sound.

"Ya see? Your big brother ain't so bad. He might even show little wuss boy how to talk like a real man one of these days." Indie wheezed, snorted, and spat all in one gurgling laugh.

The blood in my veins turned into ice water. I told myself to move, but no part of me obeyed. Birdie's hand trembled on my arm. I prayed she wouldn't crack up and start screaming like she did the time a scorpion stung me out by our windmill.

The Lobo Gas and Grocery was a family-owned business about two miles out of town. Harold and Juanita Nez, and Mrs. Nez's sister—Janet Roon—were the owners.

The thought of those nice people at the mercy of someone like Indie was terrible.

The next few minutes were so quiet, I worried the men might hear us hyperventilating above them. We needed a little noise so we could take off. We got some. Right after Indie took another drink from the bottle, he started mouthing off.

"Heh. Heh. How you gonna make that old coot vamoose?" His voice rose. "If he comes in the store, he'll be sorry. We're hitting Mexico tomorrow, and that old piece of rust better stay out of the way."

Birdie dug her fingernails into the top of my hand.

Shonnie cleared his throat. "No problem, Indie. He hunts old truck parts to resell. I'll tell him I know about a man in town who wants to junk his truck and give the parts to whoever hauls them off. First come, first serve. I'll start talking it up while we're riding to the station. Give him a fake address. He'll be in a big hurry to get there."

Now I knew for sure. The *old coot* was Mr. Nakai.

Indie erupted in a coughing fit. He set the bottle down. "Water!"

Shonnie brought a bucket and dipped something shiny into it. It looked like a can with the label peeled off. Indie drank and pitched the shiny cylinder into the dark. "My leg's cold!" he yelled. Shonnie left and returned with a covering. He snapped it open and handed it to Indie. He picked up the bottle and stepped into darkness.

I squeezed Birdie's arm. We shimmied backward a few feet and rose to our knees. I whispered, "Don't talk yet." We aimed toward Mustang Canyon. Where were the moon and stars? It was serious dark away from the firelight. I stopped.

"Birdie, we have to get the police up here."

"No lie—oh-my-gosh! He…that man is so awful." Birdie was going wacky. Any second she'd start sobbing out loud. I grabbed her shoulders.

"Listen. All we have to do is boogie off this mountain. No big deal, Birdie." Her soft cries were gaining strength. "Birdie, now stop it. We're all right, okay?"

"Uh-huh. I think so."

We wandered a few minutes. Moonlight would have been a huge help. I turned back toward Toho Rock. Blackness. Maybe it was the other way. We stumbled along like two babies learning to walk. Too much time passed for us to be back where we'd gotten out of the canyon earlier. Were we climbing? I couldn't tell if the ground slanted up, down or was level. Total darkness was mixing me up.

Birdie stumbled.

"You all right, Birdie?"

"I don't know. I can't see to…" Birdie's voice had tears in it.

"Take my hand. Should we go straight a few more feet, or jag right and then straight to get to the canyon?"

"Neither one. It's that way." Birdie lifted my hand and pointed it left. I looked behind us. The campfire light no longer existed. Where was that idiotic canyon?

I stepped in front of Birdie, still hanging onto her hand. After a couple of steps. I had an idea. "Let's find an opening in the trees and check the stars. Just because we can't see the moon doesn't mean the whole sky is overcast. You know how I read stars, Birdie. I'll find—" My front foot sank a few inches. It felt like I'd poked a hole into the earth. I tried to rock back on my other foot, but I sank lower. I stood unmoving and uncertain. Then, the ground dropped away.

I heard myself screaming. Birdie's cries melted into mine.

Earth enclosed me as I slid, tumbled, turned, and slid some more.

From somewhere, I heard Birdie yelp, but I couldn't stop sliding. Then, a sickening drop into dead space. I landed with a hard thud onto my hip. Gravel and dirt whooshed down on me, covering my body, filling my ears and eyes.

I turned my face into my cradled arms and screamed forever.

Chapter 33
The Cave

HIS WAS MY FIRST TIME to be buried alive. It scared me more than seeing *Wol-la-chee* at Weaver Rock. It was worse than being grounded from riding Smiles—more terrifying than losing Birdie as a best friend. I yelled at the ground dumping in on me. My screams disappeared into padded walls. I hid my head under my arms.

At last, except for smaller rivers of streaming grit, it grew quiet. My pounding heart was loud in the absence of sound. More than I'd ever wanted anything in my life, I wanted out of that black grave.

I shifted my top leg and sat up. Rubble ran off me in floods. The weight of my own head hurt my neck. I leaned it forward and combed through my hair with crusted fingers. Enough sand to fill a plastic grocery sack poured onto my jeans. My right hip throbbed.

Faraway, I heard a voice. I tried to answer, but no sound came out of my throat. I tried to spit. Too dry. I flipped dirt out my ears with my fingernails and tilted my head from side to side like at the pool. I was a living dirt ball.

Muffled sounds. I cupped my hands over my ears and pressed to create pressure. I fake yawned.

"Silki…Silki."

Birdie was alive! I swabbed the inside of my mouth and ears with a scarf.

"Bir…Bird…." I cleared my throat, worked up spit, and let it slide down my throat. It tasted like a sandstorm. Salty tears ran over my lips. Mixed with soil, they made my chin feel slick. "Birdie, where…are you?"

"Silki, I hear you! I'm up here."

"We're not…dead." I put my hands over my mouth and sobbed.

Be strong, Silki.

I stood, staggered, and sank back down. How big was this place? Could I fall deeper into the cavern? The silence frightened me. "Birdie?"

"I'm…on a ledge, I think. My foot's caught. I see the moon. It keeps going behind clouds."

My heart leaped. If Birdie saw sky, we probably weren't buried too deep in the ground. I force-gulped spit down my throat, ignoring the stinging dryness.

"Birdie, I'm in a cave room or something. I don't know if it drops off more, but I'll check it out," I called, massaging the stinging areas under my ear lobes.

"No! Please don't, Silki!" Birdie started wailing.

"Calm down, girl. I promise I won't fall deeper." I inched over debris and rubbed the darkness in front of me with my palms. "Please don't drop off," I whispered. I sucked in my bottom lip. Yuck—gritty.

Absolute quiet roared in my ears. I wondered how prairie dogs, ants, and gophers lived in such deep silence. Sixteen miniature steps later, my hands touched something solid. I pressed into it, straining with all my might to see. A sliver of moonlit sky appeared.

Ideas and adrenalin took over. I dropped and felt for a rock about the size of my hand. I easily found one. I started untying the simple knots in my filthy scarf chain.

"Hey, Bird, ready to get out of here?"

"What do you mean?"

"Hold on a minute while I do something." I worked my scarf ends into Double-Overhand-Stopper knots, the strongest kind Grandfather ever taught me. He said they were strong enough for mountain climbing. With no light, I had to do my work by feeling. My grubby fingers felt like claws. How far up was Birdie? I double-dogged hoped I had enough scarves to reach from me to her.

"What's going on?" Birdie asked.

"I'm throwing a rock up there with my scarves tied together. Try to wrap the end around whatever snagged your foot. Tie a strong knot—like the one I taught you last summer. Then hang on tight and don't let it go."

Birdie didn't answer.

"Hey, we're too young to be mummies—we're ditching this Egyptian tomb." That was supposed to be comical, but Birdie started bawling instead.

"Bird, we're getting out of here. Believe it."

"But we—"

I interrupted her on purpose. "Ready?" I asked in my excited voice. "Make noise so I can aim. Better cover your face."

Birdie started humming, but it was mostly crying.

I was sore, bruised, scraped, and filthier than I'd ever been in my life. My arm felt too heavy to throw a rock.

Do it anyway.

I listened to Birdie's wobbly tune, crouched, and threw. "Did I get close?"

"I didn't hear anything," she said.

The rock had landed on something solid because it didn't come back and hit me in the face. Was there a chute leading down to the cave room—like a slide? I tugged on the end of the scarf rope. Dirt and gravel showered my face as I pulled it toward me. I'd throw harder this time.

"Make sounds, girlfriend."

Birdie started singing *Girls Just Want to Have Fun.*

"Good one, Bird! Here goes."

"Ow. You smacked my leg. I'm trying to reach it. Hold on…I'm in a crazy position. Okay, the rock is in my hand."

I did an in-my-head victory dance. "Can you fasten the end to something?"

"I'm already doing it—around a big rock."

Waiting, I started thinking. What if that horrible Indie had heard us screaming? If Shonnie heard us, would he tell Indie? Maybe they were out there looking for us right now. No use to mention any of that to Birdie—she was already freaked out.

"Is it tied yet?" I asked, nervous from my thoughts.

"I keep messing up the knot."

"Wrap the rock at the end around part of a scarf two complete times. Keep it loose. Then pass the rock through the turns and pull tight."

My end of the scarf rope ripped out of my hands.

No!

My heart hammered as I batted the darkness with my hands. At last, my fingertips felt something soft. I grabbed it. "Birdie, be careful! Don't pull anymore!"

"Okay," she said. "Got it."

I was weak with relief. My scarves had never been so important. I took a deep breath, blew it out, and stood on tiptoes to get a better grip. I prayed the scarves would hold my weight. My arms were shaking before I started.

"Here I come, Birdie." I curled my body to place my feet flat against the cave wall. Right foot. Left foot. Left hand. Right hand. It was harder than I'd imagined, but the thought of falling back into that lifeless cavity below inspired me. It became my new Mission in life not to do that. I sobbed aloud several times.

"Silki, you're getting closer. Don't give up."

"I…never…give…up…I…am…strong…I…am… *Diné*." I said one word with each placement of my hand or foot. It helped take my mind off the strain. The straight wall angled into a slant—the chute. I imagined I was pulling myself up the Eagle Elementary slide with a rope.

Tiny lights exploded under my eyelids and along the sides of my eyes. They mixed with stinging sweat rolling off my forehead. I heard high-pitched ringing in my left ear. At last, my hand felt the rough edge of a jutting rock. I gritted my teeth and hauled myself over the top. I had never, ever been so tired.

"Wahoo," I panted.

"Here I am, Silki-Wilki," Birdie hadn't called me that since we were in second grade. It sounded good. I crawled toward her voice with quaking arms and legs. When I touched her hair, I collapsed. Birdie's hand patted me.

In a few minutes, I said, "Birdie?"

"Yeah?"

"Promise me we'll never do *this* adventure again."

Birdie giggled weakly. "You got it."

I looked up at the mouth of the cave. It seemed like an easy climb to the top. That is, if my abused body cooperated. When the moonlight switched on again. I tried to size up Birdie's problem. She was on her back with her head pointed toward the cave room I'd just escaped. Her tennis shoe was wedged in an awkward angle between two craggy rocks. A dark line about three inches long crossed her ankle and disappeared into the top of her shoe.

"If I untie your shoe, can you pull your foot out?"

"I think so. It's throbbing a little."

I touched her ankle with one finger. She winced. I untied her shoe and tried to ease it off her foot. She screamed.

I sat back on my heels. Birdie wasn't going anywhere. Even if I freed her foot, she couldn't put weight on it to climb out. I had to bring help, and we both knew it.

"I'll be back before you have time to miss me," I said. Birdie started to sniffle. I wanted to put my head on her shoulder and cry like a baby.

"How? What if you can't get off the mountain in the dark? You may not be back until tomorrow. And, and… what if those men find you?"

"Huh! No way. Listen, I'll be back with help faster than…well, faster than a jackrabbit at a hip-hop contest." That was pretty lame, but I wanted to make Birdie laugh. She didn't.

"I'll leave my scarves with you, except for a couple of them. I may need them, you know? Anyway, remember there's a good hard rock tied on the end."

Birdie knew what I was getting at. My stomach flip-flopped at the thought of leaving her helpless and trapped in a ground hole. Criminals were on the mountain. Wild animals hunted at night. Not to mention *Wol-la-chee.*

Sheep Shears, I hadn't thought of Him for at least an hour. Or about *Operation: Back Off!* Or even about being mad at Birdie. All that seemed like years ago.

"Silki, I have to tell you something—"

I reached down, felt for Birdie's hand and squeezed it. "We'll talk until we throw up when we get home, okay?"

Birdie squeezed my hand back. "You're a pinion nut."

My heart was in my throat as I climbed my way to the top. Even though my body was beat to powder, I was above ground in a few minutes.

"I'll be right back," I called down the cave opening in a medium-loud voice. I thought I heard Birdie answer, but I wasn't sure. I looked around. How did it get so dark again? Where was that ornery moon? No stars either, and it smelled like rain.

Oh great—I was worried about Birdie. Now I was worried about me too.

Chapter 34
Bad Luck

CONCHO MOUNTAIN was as dark as *Wol-la-chee's* heart. I stumbled around in different directions, but nothing seemed right. I doubted my decisions. Was I going in circles? I sank to the ground and hung my head.

I was so far beyond starved and thirsty. Worse, my heart was miserable with my own foolishness. Birdie and I shouldn't have gone to Toho Rock. Whose fault was that? Mine. Who stepped into the cave hole? Me. I banged my forehead up and down on my knee.

Why couldn't the clouds just roll away and let the night lights do their duty?

What time was it? I lifted my head and saw a faint red glow far below me. Toho Rock again? Impossible. But what else could it be?

Hope flickered like a candle. From Toho Rock, I could start over. I made myself rethink the path Birdie and I took from Mustang Canyon to Toho Rock. I mentally counted the steps and concentrated on the angles. Now all I had to do was reverse those moves. My poor brain was turning into soup, but I knew I could do it this time.

The slight blush of light became my beacon. I stepped lightly, testing the ground so I didn't wind up in another earth hole. At last, I stood in the trees above Toho Rock. Were the two strangers where they ought to be? Did they hear our screams? I had to know.

I crept to the rim of Toho Rock and peeked over the edge. Indie was wrapped up cocoon style. The melted bowl of embers spread a ginger-red shadow over Shonnie's outline. Whew—both men were asleep. Now I could do my reverse moves back to the canyon without thinking they might get me.

I started counting. First step. Second step. Angle a little to the right. Step…my foot froze above the ground. Something wasn't right.

A presence!

My airborne leg started to shake. I set it down. Both legs started wobbling. Sweat popped through the sludge cake on my face. Heat flowed down my back like hot lava. So this was how it would end—*Wol-la-chee* attacking me, and my screams waking the bad guys. Who would destroy me the worst?

Movement.

A low animal growl raised the hair right off my head. I stepped backward and heard a wet throat hiss. Another unsure step and my ankle turned. I fell over sideways. Sharp cactus spikes pierced my arm. I pictured a whole village of angry fairies attacking my arm with flaming torches.

How could I stifle my cries? I needed to fill the entire dark sky with screams of pain. I clamped a hand over my mouth and rose up on my heels. I lost my balance and fell backward onto something hard—a rock. It shifted.

It began to free-slide. I grabbed onto the sides.

I rode the rock like a backward sled down a wave of elastic sand, right down the center of Toho Rock. Down, down I went, in something like fast-slow motion. Nothing about it seemed real—except the landing—which jarred an airy whimper out of me.

I was less than four feet from Indie's head. In the orangey light, I saw his eyes flutter open. They simmered with fierceness.

Run!

I couldn't.

"What the h—l!" he snarled, groping the ground for something. He jumped to his feet waving a pipe in the air. He bounced toward me like a crazed baboon, raising the pipe over my head.

Chapter 35

Clearly, Scorpius

SAILED BACKWARD with gargantuan force. The air hissed out of me like a punctured inner tube. I couldn't see. "Indie! No!" boomed a voice over my head.

"Move you little worm!" Indie's voice was thick. He cursed. "I said—"

"No! This is a sign. Good medicine! Listen to me!"

I felt cracked and spread out like an egg in a skillet. Shonnie's chest clamped tighter over my head until I thought I was smothering. Except for gasping for air, I didn't dare move. Indie roared in the background like an angry lion. Above me, Shonnie's voice dropped to a soothing, rhythmic tone.

"Great luck, Indie. Any problems crossing the border tomorrow—she's our ticket out. We can dump her on the other side."

Indie's sounds were muffled. Shonnie's were calming.

"I'll tie her up…get some painkiller for your leg. You probably hurt yourself jumping up like that. I'll take care of everything. This is real fortune—like she fell out of the sky just for tomorrow." Shonnie chuckled softly and kept talking in a singsong voice.

I was going to be sick. I struggled. Shonnie moved away, and I dry heaved. When I stopped gagging, Shonnie handed me a shiny can. "It's water," he said, his face close to mine. I sipped and handed the can back to him, too upset to swallow. He withdrew into the darkness, returned with a liquor bottle, and placed it in Indie's open hand.

Shonnie pointed for me to come closer to the embers. I thought about making a run for it. He shot me a warning look. I limped to where he pointed and sat.

"Don't let her get away, Shonnie! What is she, a mountain goat? Probably stinks. Throw one of them buckets of water on her." Indie's cackle was ugly.

I wanted to jump on that lump of no-good man and claw his face off. Shonnie ignored him and disappeared into the shadows. He came back carrying a short rope. He knelt and noticed the cactus thorns sticking out of my arm.

"Want those out?" he asked

"Uh…I…guess so."

He left, returned with pliers. I bit the back of my hand while he worked the hooked needle ends out of my flesh. Silent tears dripped off my face.

"The fuzzy ones have to work themselves out. They'll itch and blister first." Shonnie said. He bound my ankles with unwasted motions and reached for the scarves tied around my neck. I clamped my hands over them. "Don't make this hard on yourself," he said in a low voice. Even in the dim light, I thought his eyes were kind. I dropped my hands.

I didn't recognize the knots he used to tie my hands, but I vowed to find a way to wiggle out of them later. No way were criminals taking me on a journey of crime or across the Mexican border.

I tried to make eye contact with Shonnie, but he wouldn't look at me. He stirred the coals and dropped several skinny sticks on top. He stretched and checked his watch.

"That old man rolls down the road about seven, Indie. Plenty of time. Drink up. Want something to eat?"

"Shut up, mama's boy. First, you whine about my booze. Then, you act like it's Kool-Aid," Indie said, lifting the bottle and swigging with gusto. "Don't tell me what to do." He mumbled in broken Navajo for a few seconds and made other noises that didn't make sense.

"You're a stupid loser," he muttered a few minutes later.

He sucked on his bottle like a nursing calf and broke into a brainless song about some bottles of beer on the wall. He spat at the end of it. He drank the last drops with the bottle upside down on his lips. He tried to throw it, but it rolled out of his limp hand.

I stared at Indie spellbound. Never had I seen or heard anything like him, even in a zoo. He swayed like a cobra curling out of a basket, pointing a trembling hand at me.

"Donneh try eslaping. Swonnie Bloy shed you fell outa da shy. Did you frawl out da..." He slumped over in the sand. Shonnie walked over and picked up the bottle.

My chance had come. I was betting on Shonnie being at least half-good.

"Shonnie, can you and I talk a little?"

"My name is *Sean*."

"I'm so sorry. Sean, can you please, please not hurt the Nezes or their sister tomorrow?" Sean's face scrunched up like he was in pain. He poked at a fizzing branch in the fire with the drinking end of Indie's bottle.

"You know about that?"

"Oh not very much. I just know the Nezes are really nice, and they help lots of other people who need it. And my best friend Birdie is in mortal danger right now. She's hurt. We fell in a cave, and I climbed out, but her foot is trapped and her ankle's probably broken. She needs a doctor. And I almost got attacked a few minutes ago." I gestured at the rim with my lips. "Now isn't that creepy—a mountain lion or a panther trying to make me their midnight snack? No wonder this place is called Toho Rock. *Toho* is Hopi for 'mountain lion,' you know."

I wanted to shut up, but I couldn't.

"And mountain lions aren't the only creatures to worry about out there in the dark." I drew in a long draft of air. "Believe me, Shonnie, er, uh, Sean, there are some things about this mountain you don't even want to know. You're not safe either. But it's no place for a girl to be trapped in a cave. Can you imagine my poor Birdie? I know you're not really a bad person. Your eyes say so. Please let me go, Shonnie…I mean Sean."

Sean eased to the ground without taking his eyes off me. He criss-crossed his legs and kept staring. I guessed my habit of nervous babbling stole his words.

"So, will you…let me go?" I put on my best pleading face. Would it work with all the dirty glop on my face?

Sean exhaled noisily and looked away. "I can't do that, Silki."

"You…you know my name?"

"I know lots of things. I know I won't let you get hurt."

My stomach did somersaults. How did this stranger know me? I'd never seen him or his loser brother before tonight.

Sean stared into the flames. I studied his silhouette. I couldn't help mentally sketching him. Was he a bad person, or was he just making bad decisions? I had to find out. "You're nothing like your brother, Sean."

No answer.

"I'll bet you really don't like being a criminal, do you? Maybe you're at one of those forks in the road my Father talks about. You know, where you make decisions that make you who you are for the rest of your life."

Sean leaped up like he'd been stung on the rump. He shoved his hands in his pockets, walked around the fire a couple of times, stopped, and looked up at the sky. Finally, he sighed like he was the most exhausted person on the planet. Then, he started talking.

"Indie—*Terence* is his real name—we're half-brothers. Indie's mother had terrible drug problems. She was full of poison, and she poured it into her son his whole life. He's…bad. You can't grasp how…anyway, I've done some crap I'm not proud of, but at least no one else got hurt."

"I think I get it, Sean." I waited.

Sean sat down. "He showed up at our door, bleeding and acting crazy. Dad tried to run him off, but Indie went ballistic—worse than he'd ever been before. He slugged our dad twice with that pipe. I don't know if my father is alive or…" Sean pounded his fist into his forehead.

I thought about Father's conversation with Lt. Jake at the fairgrounds. Was Indie the thief who robbed the pawnshop, got shot, and left blood outside the store? I already knew he was the bully who clobbered a man in his own home and put him in a coma. Sean had to be the missing minor. To think of someone hurting his own father short-circuited my human wiring. It was unthinkable. Sean's voice cut into my thoughts.

"Indie needed a slave, a thief, to do everything for him while his leg healed. I have to help him cross the border to Mexico tomorrow or he'll…he threatened to kill my Aunt Sooz."

Poor Sean. He was more of a prisoner than I was. I had to help him escape. "Don't you see, Sean? This is your chance for justice."

He stared up at the sky.

"Indie should pay for his crimes," I said.

Sean didn't move.

"Sean?"

It was like he came out of a trance. He sprang from the ground so fast, I thought he was attacking me. My breath caught in my throat as he dropped to the ground by my feet. He untied my ankles, then my hands. I stood up rubbing my wrists and keeping a watchful eye on him. He kicked sand over the fire.

"Uh, could you bring something to discourage mountain lions?" I asked.

He parted his jacket to reveal a knife tucked into the top of his jeans.

"What about Indie?"

Sean grunted. "He's out cold."

We evaporated into the darkness. Crickets and other night bugs sang to us as we climbed up and away from Toho Rock. It didn't smell like rain anymore. I looked up. The brightest cluster in the sky winked down at me—clearly, Scorpius. "This way," I said, wild and free again under the twinkling starlight.

Chapter 36

Some Are Evil And Some Are Good

A LIT-UP SKY CHANGES everything. I led us straight to Mustang Canyon. Why couldn't it have been this starry bright when Birdie and I left Toho Rock the first time? Then Birdie wouldn't be hanging upside down in a cave.

When Sean told me it was ten thirty, I almost croaked. It seemed like I'd been on Concho Mountain several days. Now I wanted to bring the whole Navajo Nation police force, doctors, helicopters, and maybe ninjas to arrest Indie and rescue Birdie. Well, maybe not ninjas.

We passed the split in Mustang Canyon and were making good time down the north side of Twin I toward Red Rocks. I was ignoring my pain as a sacrifice for Birdie. I knew how lonely and scared she was right now. Nearing Weaver Rock, uneasiness washed over me. I put on my brakes.

"What's up?" Sean asked.

"Weaver Rock."

"Weaver Rock?"

"Yeah. It's where the rock fairies dance when the moon is…oh, never mind." That sounded ridiculous right now. "It was one of my favorite places until something horrible ruined it."

"Hmm. Well, we'd better keep moving," he said.

"Just a second, Sean," I said, squatting. Something was happening to me. My shivers were turning into shakes. I felt too worn-out to be brave like Nick anymore.

Sean crouched beside me. "Silki, do you know how Indie and I found this mountain? We started out in my dad's truck. Indie ditched it the second day because it was traceable. We spotted an old man filling up his truck at that Lobo gas station. The back end had a tarp, so Indie and I climbed inside. After a bumpy ride, the guy pulled over and lifted the hood to check his engine. He parked by this mountain. Indie and I sneaked out the back."

This wasn't a social gathering. Why was Sean telling me all this?

"The heavy trees on the east side made a good hiding place. I pushed for it because I didn't want Indie hurting the old man. He was crazy with pain. And for booze. I wouldn't let him have any until we found somewhere to settle. It was hard getting him up here, especially with his big mouth. He never shut up about what he'd do if anyone came snooping around."

I wanted Sean to be quiet. *Wol-la-chee* might attack any minute. I wanted to jump up and run home, but I was rusted into a knot. "Sean," I whispered, "I don't mean to be rude, but we're in a very dangerous place right now. I can't explain *Wol-la-chee* to you. Nobody but Birdie and I even know He exists."

"*Wol-la-chee*? Doesn't that mean *ant*?"

My teeth started chattering. "It's our c-code n-n-ame for the Ancient Ant M-m-an. He was right here at Wea-v-ver Rock. He's awful—like Indie. All w-e-e did was k-k-keep some old relics fr-fr-om an anthill. I gave most of them back and tried to help Him get *h-hozho*…but He didn't care. He-he's probably listening to us right n-now, Sean," I stammered. My teeth sounded like false teeth clacking.

At last, I had told someone besides Birdie about *Wol-la-chee*. It felt almost wonderful, until Sean moaned. Was he getting scared too?

"Whoa, dude…" Sean muttered. "When did you see this ant guy, Silki?"

I counted back in my head and tried to speak. "Ex-ac-ac-actly three w-w-eeks ago. He f-f-f-flew…or l-leaped off a l-l-ledge—"

"Feathers?"

"Huh?"

"Was he covered in feathers?"

"Y-yeah."

"He yelled really loud?"

How did Sean know that? My heart flip-flopped. Ideas blew around my mind like trash gusting across a dump. They churned up, down, and crossways. They settled, creating a monster I couldn't handle. Trancelike, I asked the question I never wanted answered.

"When did you and Indie come...to Concho Mountain?"

"Three weeks ago."

A glacier sucking me into its frozen center couldn't have shocked me more than the icy truth kneeling beside me.

Sean was *Wol-la-chee.*

I ran.

"Wait!" Sean called behind me.

"Get away!" I screamed, bursting into tears. "I hate you!"

I passed by Weaver Rock and let out another round of blazing mad screeches. The trickery...the deception...the fear. It was too much.

Sean's hands grabbed me.

I fought back like a rabid mountain lion. "Let go of me, you...you lunatic! You're evil—just like Indie! Where'd you get your costume?" I coated the word *costume* with mockery because no Navajo called real ceremonial or dance clothing a costume.

"Coward! So brave...scaring girls! And you pushed me! No one pushes me!" I released a scorcher scream. "I'll take you down—"

We wrestled. Sean quickly gained the lead. His arms surrounded me, squeezing the air from my world. He stuffed something in my mouth and wrapped it around my head. I fought for my freedom with everything I ever believed in.

"Holy crap! Your screams could wake the real Ancients. Listen to me!"

I couldn't. Rage controlled me. I kicked, squirmed, and muffle-yelled against the wad in my mouth.

"Silki, stop! Indie's a career criminal, not a normal person. Don't you get what that means?"

I kicked behind me at Sean's legs. He leaned and ducked. We struggled in a circle.

"Just listen! Indie may be fifty percent Navajo, but he's one-hundred percent *not Diné.*"

I tried to jab my right elbow under his nose. Then my left elbow. Sean dodged my hits. I kicked harder at his legs. He spoke to me in breathy fragments.

"Indie has no mercy…no value for… life…Silki, knock it off! He understands…prison life…more than…the real world. The day I saw you…and your horse…on the mountain…all I thought about was what…Indie said he'd do to snoopers. I saved you, Silki."

I stopped fighting and stood still.

"After Indie beat my dad, he told me to grab my stuff pronto or he'd smash Dad's head in some more. He was stomping through the house cursing us and yelling threats. I was raw with hatred for my so-called brother."

Sean loosened his grip.

"My father is…was…I don't know, a man of wisdom with many talents. I stuffed some of his ceremonial regalia into his huge duffle bag. I don't know why—to keep him with me, I guess. I took his favorite old hat too, and a handful of turquoise nuggets from his jewelry supplies. I even grabbed things he'd saved in a wooden box from when I was young. Like my first deck of cards. I was… delirious. Indie was destroying our lives and everything I cared about."

Vague images took shape in my mind.

"I think I tried to carry my life in that duffle bag. I've lost most of it now. I used it as trade because I had to…to steal for us to live. By leaving something behind, I didn't feel as bad. I…hate what I did." Sean's voice was thick.

"The day after I set up our camp by that awesome rock, I scouted the whole mountain. It's not big, so I covered it quick. I found some unusual things and used them for trading," he said.

Like my earring and Grandmother's old photograph.

"About noon, I saw a beautiful paint horse ground tied at the bottom of the north side. I heard you calling to him from the top of that stack of red rocks. You were so free. I envied you. But what if Indie had seen you? Even injured, he's someone you don't want to tangle with."

I swallowed hard.

"I ran back to camp. Indie was fevered, cursing— delusional. I gave him some beers I stole right before we came back to the Rez. Booze is the only thing that keeps him controlled. I rigged up a crazy outfit to scare you away until we went to Mexico. I hoped it would work. It was a huge risk. For all I knew, you'd come back with the men in your family, or the cops.

Why didn't I? Birdie's accusations that I lived in an imaginary world were cutting me like sharp scissors.

"After that, I saw you lots of places. At the high school, someone pushed double doors into my legs. When I saw it was you, I ducked into a side door. You gave me some big bruises that day."

I smacked *Wol-la-chee*?

"One time you were pulling plants and digging roots with an elderly woman, but you didn't come any closer than the foothills. I almost let you see me that time you were playing a game and dumping things on a giant anthill by the red boulders. Right before I gave you another reason to stay away, I heard men talking in the orchard and took off."

I was in a stupor listening to Sean. My whole world as I'd imagined it this summer didn't exist. It was only air. I nodded, and Sean dropped his arms. I took the wad out of my mouth. Even in the dark, I knew it was my missing tangerine scarf.

"I didn't mean to be your worst nightmare, Silki. I just couldn't risk Indie getting his hands on you." Sean breathed out a weary sigh. "I don't know why some people are good and some are evil, but it just happens sometimes. My father said Indie's *life wind* had turned dark."

I knew that wasn't good.

Faint shouts and whistles floated up the mountainside. "Silki! Birdie! Hey Ho! Woo-a-woo! Ho Hey!"

I chewed on a fingernail. It tasted like mud. This was a moment like no other in my whole life. How could I, Silki, be standing in the moonlight with the actual *Wol-la-chee*?

Sean dropped his head. I took his hand.

"Ready?" I asked.

Chapter 37
Flight or Fight

EAN SCRAMBLED EASILY UP the side of Mustang Canyon. I followed. He lowered a helpful hand to me. Before I touched it, his shadowy form slid away like a bead on an abacus rod.

A tarantula shape draped over him. The sounds of punches and airy gasps filled the air. Sean and his attacker rolled into the canyon in a ball. I slid back to the bottom with my pulse racing. The sour odor of liquor and sweat hit my nostrils.

Indie!

My screams had awakened a passed-out drunk? My fault again. Now it was time to put my big mouth to good use. I raised my shoulders to load my lungs with maximum air and screamed as I'd never screamed before. I did it again. Indie's face sneered at me in the moonlight.

"You're next," he growled.

Sean escaped from Indie's grasping bulk. "Run!" he shouted as his form crumpled like a piece of paper under his half-brother's vicious tackle.

Staring at the terrible scene before me, I knew I was at another fork in my road. I could run away like the wind, or...

I found what I wanted. Shallow roots ripped away as I wrestled it loose from its earthy home. It was heavy. I swayed under the weight as I shuffled toward the battle.

The moon snuck behind the clouds. I waited. The grunts of struggle and a lonesome night wren naming stars made an unworldly mixture of sound.

The seconds ticked by slowly, and my sore arm muscles quivered.

Be calm. Aim well.

I welcomed the advice in my head this time.

The moon eased from behind a dappled cloud blanket and reflected off the metal pipe aimed for Sean's skull. I shrieked my most excellent war cry and rushed toward Indie, hurling the rock at his head with all my might. Definitely a ten plus on my *Good Reactions Scale!*

Indie howled as Sean slipped out from underneath him. He staggered to his feet and snaked toward me holding his head. He pointed and opened his mouth, but no words came out. A second later, he toppled like a sawed-down Ponderosa pine.

"Don't you ever come to our land again!" I bellowed at the figure whimpering on the sand. I let all my fear and fury fill up that one big, yelled-out sentence. It felt incredible to get it out.

Men clamored down the sides of the canyon like ants claiming a half-eaten jelly doughnut.

"Silki!" My father opened his arms wide. I threw myself around his neck.

Chapter 38

Lost and Found

LIGHTS FLICKERED DOWN the side of north Twin I. I pulled the blanket tighter around me and leaned into Father. He patted the top of my head. A horse snorted behind us. Standing at the base of Red Rocks with armed police officers and the Saddle Rescue Team was surreal.

Several of the men knew about the ground cave on Twin II, so I didn't have to go back up the mountain with them to get Birdie. Truthfully, I had no idea where she was.

Indie had been handcuffed, half-carried, half-dragged off the mountain and put into the back of a police van. I still saw the van's red rear lights bouncing through the peach tree branches.

"You gave that dude an honest knot on his head, young lady," Lt. Jake said, coming to stand beside us. "Yeah, that's real good—he's got a rap sheet bigger than those rocks." He nodded toward Red Rocks. "He won't be visiting us here anymore, not unless he plans to live to one hundred.

Going into maximum security. He had a pistol on him for that robbery up in Shiprock. Yeah…our *federales* don't take to that kind of stuff with his felony history. Bad hombre. They'll throw away the key this time."

"Hmmph," Father said, rocking forward, then back on his boot heels. He still didn't like crime discussed in front of me. That was pretty funny since I'd been on a mountain all night with a hunted criminal. My dad was just too sweet.

Flares, headlights, and flashlights made it easy to see the outline of Sean's head and shoulders in the backseat of Lt. Jake's Chevy SUV. He wasn't under arrest. I'd explained how he saved my life and had been Indie's prisoner. Earlier, Lt. Jake called Shiprock to check on Sean's father. Now Sean was waiting for information to come.

I knew that wasn't the only reason he wanted to be alone. He was embarrassed. He'd stolen, deceived, and almost become a real robber. It was understandable since it kept his half-brother from harming innocent people. Still, it made him ashamed. That's just the way our people are wired.

The lights flashing through the trees meant Birdie was out of danger. I handed the blanket to Father and walked as fast as I could across the lower rise of a foothill. When the stretcher and four men appeared through the cedars, I broke into a limping run.

The first thing I noticed was a giant paddle splint sticking up in the air. Birdie's right foot was somewhere inside it. Dirt clods and weed stalks hung in her hair like ornaments. Her grimy face and arms flashed me back to when we used to play for hours in the red muddy roads after our August rainstorms. It was a good thing my Auntie Jane wasn't there—she couldn't take so much yucky mess all at once.

"You look pretty good, Bird," I fibbed, walking alongside the stretcher in between Mr. Yazzee and Birdie's cousin Mark.

Birdie wrinkled her nose. "Sure, Silk. I'm Miss Rez Universe."

"Then I'm Miss Navajo America!" I said, patting my dirty cheeks. In the middle of our grins, Birdie's expression changed.

"I was afraid for you alone on the mountain," she said.

"Nah," I said, shrugging my shoulders. You shouldn't have been. Besides, you know me—I made you a promise."

"Yes, I do know you," Birdie said, staring past my eyes and into my soul. And just like that, something changed between us. Birdie and I connected as young women, not as girls. It was breathtaking.

Birdie handed me my scarves with the rock still tied to the end. "They need special care."

"Definitely a job for Auntie Jane," I said, lifting them with two fingers like they were polluted.

Birdie giggled. "Did you have trouble finding the canyon in the dark?" she asked.

I put my hand over my mouth and laughed silently. I felt like I'd lived at least a year since I left Birdie in the ground a few hours ago. "Oh, a little."

"So the bad guys are going to jail?"

I gave her a thumbs-up. I could explain it all to her later. Birdie motioned for me to hunker down. In my ear she said, "What about *Wol-la-chee*?"

"Oh, wow, Bird. He's long gone."

"Huh? Really?"

Birdie's expression should have been framed and hung on the wall.

"Trust me, girl, it's the story of the year. I'll have to start it from, you know, the creation of the earth. But right now, you have to go the hospital for x-rays," I said.

The smile on Birdie's dirty face sent me soaring through the night sky. "See you tomorrow," I said.

"Promise?"

"Triple-dog."

I stopped, and the men carrying Birdie passed me by. Birdie looked over her shoulder at me and made a peace sign in the air. For the first time, I made one back.

Rescuers walked by leading horses to trailers. Vehicles backed up, turned around, pulled out. All the commotion flung a fine, sandy dust into the atmosphere that resembled mist. An SUV pulled alongside me.

"Get in, honey. Jake's driving us back to the house," Father said, leaning over from the passenger side. He looked tired.

I went around to the door behind Father. The bright light from the open door hurt my eyes. I squinted at Sean propped against the other door fumbling with his cap in his lap. I gasped. I slid into the seat beside him and told myself I had to be hallucinating from exhaustion and hunger. What I thought I saw just couldn't be.

"Sean?"

"Yeah?"

"Where are you from?

"Shiprock mostly."

"You lived there long?"

"About five years."

"Your mother lives there too?" Sean didn't answer. I knew I was behaving boldly—even rudely—for a Navajo girl, but I couldn't help it. We'd be at my house in a few minutes.

"Sean, your mom…?"

"She…she left when I was three. My parents divorced."

"She left you?"

"I stayed with my dad and his sister, my Aunt Sooz. My mother is…she passed away a few years ago."

I knew I was treading on Sean's private property, but it was the only way.

Lt. Jake's radio spurted out a blob of static. He picked up. "Yeah? When? Uh-huh. Right. We're on our way to the station in a few. Over.

"Sean, we have a missing person's report filed on you from Shiprock. Your family's been looking for you. One of my officers just spoke to your dad. He and…uh, an aunt, I think, are on their way to Mesa Redondo tonight. Your dad's okay. Looks like things are working out pretty good, son," Lt. Jake said.

"Thank you, sir. *Ahéhee*." Sean's voice quivered. I patted his arm to let him know I was glad about his father.

Oh-my-gosh. Imagine me comforting *Wol-la-chee*. *The Most Bizarre Summer of my Life* didn't begin to describe this night.

The charged scene opening up in front of us stole my attention. Our place was lit up like a full-blown night rodeo. Pickups and police vehicles parked in a fan shape on the gravel outside our house. Trucks hugged the sides of the road. Rescue-team riders gathered in groups or sat on horses. Family, neighbors, and people I didn't even recognize were everywhere. Sparks from an open fire in the yard columned into the sky. Smudgy white steam rose from the spouts of a gigantic SpatterWare coffee pot and several smaller pots on a grill over the fire pit.

"Unbee-leeve-able," I said.

I forced my thoughts back to my new Mission inside the vehicle. It was now or never.

"Sean, are you an only child?"

"Huh? Why do you want to know?"

"Well, are you?"

"Silki...some things are best left to the past."

"I'm sorry, Sean, but this is important."

Lt. Jake angled the SUV into a slot in front of a Ford Bronco. I teetered on the edge of the seat with both heels bouncing up and down on the floorboard. I plunged forward into unknown territory.

"Okay, let me say it like this…do you know where your sister is?"

He hesitated a second before answering. "No. We lost contact."

"One more thing…what color are your eyes?"

"What? Crap, Silki, I—"

"Please?" I begged.

"Green. They're green. Now, stop—"

The doors up front opened, flooding the inside of the SUV. I stared at Sean's reddish-brown wavy hair. Around his neck, he wore a silver-dollar-sized medallion with a design I didn't need to see. I already knew it matched the design Geri doodled and painted on her perfectly manicured nail. After all, she was his sister.

Chapter 39

In Beauty May I Walk
Hozógo nasádo

HE TOYOTA SIENNA made a half circle and stopped a few feet from Birdie's front gate. In unison, five doors opened. Girls sprang from every opening except the driver's door. The driver stepped out in a cap and a shiny red and yellow jacket. He waved, shook the travel out of his legs, and shoved his hands in his jeans.

Grandmother and Mrs. Anna paused in their conversation across one of the food-loaded portable tables set up under the stars. Everyone turned to watch Birdie's volleyball team move toward the front yard in a quiet swarm.

Birdie left my side to greet them. They gathered around her and her crutches like a hula-hoop. I backed out of the light and leaned against the side of the Yazzee's house to watch and think.

Meats sizzled and smoked on the grates over the open fire. Mother and Aunt Susan wove in and out of the invited guests like threads on a loom. Father stood in the center of an all-male group, including Mr. Tso and Cousin TeeShirt. They talked and laughed up at the sky clutching steaming cups of coffee.

In a corner of the yard, Grandfather and Mr. Nakai talked from each side of a bumper standing on its end. It was probably from Father's old truck. I shook my head. Leave it to those two guys to haggle on a night like this.

I supposed we were celebrating just about everything this evening. Grandfather said it was a Celebration of a Celebration—whatever that meant. Mostly, everyone was grateful that a criminal could do no one else harm. Birdie and I were getting a lot of credit for that; and truthfully, we didn't mind one bit.

Not that we didn't get into trouble for climbing the south side of Twin I, going to Toho Rock, and staying out after dark—we did. But afterward, Mother said so much good had come from the whole affair that it far outweighed the bad. She said Birdie and I had *walked in beauty* that night.

For *Diné*, that meant everything was in harmony and had a positive result, or something like that. She must have been right because Birdie's ankle was sprained, not broken. As for me, I just had rock burns, minor cuts, total-body bruise, stomach scrape, cactus spine punctures, a swollen tongue, and an ear infection from cave dirt. Little things like that.

Indie's life of crime was over, and Geri was reunited with her family.

Overall, pretty beautiful stuff when you thought about it.

Geri and Sean were amazed to find each other, and Geri told me she was *totally exuberant* about getting re-acquainted with her father and aunt. A very *California* way to say it, I thought. But good.

Geri promised she'd stay here for college, and I knew Nick would be happy about that. Me too, actually. She said Sean could join her in a few years after high school. In the meantime, Shiprock wasn't that far away.

Father told me Geri's dad, Mr. Bitso, came to Mesa Redondo for a jewelry expo when I was four years old. He took me to see the Kelly green shamrock surrounded by white feathers painted on the side of Mr. Bitso's truck, and he said it mesmerized me.

Stuff like that made me believe the Navajo Nation was really a cozy place, even with more than 200,000 people living in it.

"What are you doing over here, Silki?" Manny stood looking up at me with his feet apart and his hands full of potato chips.

"Just thinking about beauty, Manny. All kinds. Hey, thanks for telling your parents where to search for us the other night. But, listen, it's not nice to eavesdrop at keyholes and on top of porch roofs."

"I know. Sometimes I can't help it. You and Birdie have all the fun." He glanced over his shoulder at a line of boys his age running along the fence chasing girls about the same age. "See ya, Silki," he said, breaking into a gallop.

I studied the bright, starry canopy above me. It seemed to me that friendship was a lot like the sky—forever changing in color and shape, but always the same big sky. Take Birdie and me. No matter what we became in life, we would always be the same girls deep down where it counted. Like Grandmother and Mrs. Anna were. They were living proof that nothing rips apart true friendship.

"Where are you, Silki?" Birdie called softly from the edge of the steps. She spotted me and hobbled over. "My friends want to meet you."

I pointed at the food table. "Look over there. Can you believe our grandmothers? They never stop laughing. We're almost real relatives now, aren't we?" I said, clapping in Barbie-sized hand claps in front of my face.

Birdie giggled. "You crack me up."

"By the way, Grandmother said she and Mrs. Anna didn't invite you to hear the Two Grey Hills legend because they were making me responsible for telling you myself. They knew we weren't getting along anymore."

"That-is-awesome," Birdie said.

"They helped heal us, and we helped heal them," I said. "And I can't believe our parents never told us anything about it."

"Gah, no lie. Talk about keeping secrets," Birdie said.

"You know, this whole summer has been nothing but *firsts* for me, Birdie. I haven't figured them all out yet, but I know I'm not the same girl I was when school let out."

Birdie shook her head. "Me neither. Um, I have something to tell you. It's what I was trying to do the other day when we were on the mountain."

"Oh-my-gosh. Until you told me Tito was coming back home, I wouldn't have listened if you'd blasted my eardrum with a bullhorn. I was so mad at you and the whole world."

"Hey, you had tons of scary junk to deal with. I feel bad I was no help. And about how I was treating you like crud. You were my best friend, but I kept taking all my weird feelings out on you. Anyway, while *Nali* and I were in Santa Fe over the Fourth, I started bawling, especially for how I treated you at the corral that morning I went to camp. I couldn't stop crying for like, I don't know…all day. Your sad eyes haunted me."

I almost started blubbering.

"*Nali* said it was normal for girls our age to act strange. She said we all act porpestrous, uh, preposerous…"

"Preposterous?"

"Yeah, that's it. She said we act like that sometimes and don't even have a clue. It's because we're almost women. Hormones and all that jazz. But, I'm really sorry, Silki. You didn't deserve my mean spirit."

I took a breath so deep it left me fresh from my toes to my nose.

"So, will you forgive me?" Birdie asked.

I clucked my tongue. "You know it, girl." We both grinned ear-to-ear.

"There's something I need to tell you too, Birdie." This wasn't going to be easy, but it was the right thing to do. I cleared my throat. "Listen, you were right. I've…lived in my wild imagination way too much. I guess I forgot how to know the truth from my own head stories."

"No, Silki, that's just you. You're creative."

"But it causes major problems sometimes. Look, at some point, I should have suspected real people instead of an Ancient Being jumping through a time barrier. My *real* and *unreal* got all jumbled up.

"Birdie, I have to know. Did you ever believe in *Wol-la-chee*?"

Birdie grabbed her throat like she was choking herself. "Are you kidding, chick? Why do you think I stayed away from you so much? Even when I came back from Santa Fe, I couldn't handle it. I was a big, stupid coward. Oh, yeah, I believed! I hid out every way I could."

Hearing that felt amazing.

"We should get back to our company," Birdie said. A few steps later, she stopped and put her hand on my arm.

"Please don't stop all your wacky stories and ideas, Silk. We have a long way to go before we grow up."

"You think we might shrivel up and blow away from boredom?"

"You got it."

We both laughed. "Maybe I'll keep a few, if you insist," I said.

"I do. Come on." She pulled me into the center of her chattering teammates.

"Hi, Silki, I'm Emily. Smiles must be so pretty. I love his name," a girl with dark blond hair said. That started a vocal stampede from the rest of the girls.

"Your scarves are amazing. Birdie said you have at least fifty."

"Did you really clobber a criminal with a big rock?

"Weren't you scared, Silki?"

"Are you a barrel racer? I always wanted to do that."

"Are you and Birdie in the Celebration Circle Dancers this fall?"

"Birdie says you two were almost friends in the womb. That's so cool!"

I raised a brow and eye-pleaded for help from Birdie. She shrugged, shook her head *no*, and grinned. The glow of pride in her eyes told me everything.

≫ The End ≪

Silki, the girl of many Scarves

CANYON OF DOOM

Stealing money isn't the aim of the Mesa Redondo bank robbers. No way. They want the mysterious metal object Silki and her best friend Birdie discovered in the bogs at Canyon Daacha. With Birdie headed up to Kayenta for the rest of the summer, Silki navigates wide-eyed and solo through a whirl of thievery, scary characters, lost artifacts, and a shadowy stranger Silki dubs "Amber Eyes." Against a backdrop of Monsoon season floods and quicksand, Silki's plight is complicated by the hateful slurs of a rebellious cousin her family must rescue before it's too late. Soon, Silki finds herself smack dab in the middle of a plot stretching all the way back to World War II and reaching right into the very soul of her own family.

Coming in 2012

Glossary

Ahéhee' – (ah-heh-heh-eh) thank you.

Anglo – a Caucasian; non-Native; also *Bilagaana* (bill-uh-ghan-uh).

Angora Goat – a mohair-producing goat with a curly, wavy, or silky coat. Angoras are smaller than most other types of goats. Both males and females have horns. Coats can be white, grey, black, brown, or red with strong, elastic fibers that are different from sheep wool because of the texture and shine.

Navajo Angora Goats (NAGs) – closely related to a primitive type of Angora goat brought to the United States from Turkey in the 1840s. They are hardy, good mothers to their young, and have less hair on their faces, legs, and feet—making them less prone to tangling in brush or briars. NAGs have different colors and patterns in their coats, as well as greaseless or light oil in their fiber (fleece), making it easier to spin.

Atoo' – mutton stew.

AWOL – Military term; Absent Without Leave (i.e., gone without permission).

Bá ntseeshdá – fed up; unable to take anymore.

Brush Arbor (or Summer Arbor) – a stand-alone structure, or one that is built onto a house or hogan to provide shade and a wind-cooling effect. Arbors are commonly made of wood with an open, webbed top. The top can be metal, brush, or many other materials.

Chindi – the part of a deceased person's spirit that is out of harmony with the Navajo Way.

Churro Sheep – the first domestic sheep brought to America by the Spanish more than 400 years ago.

> **Navajo-Churro** – sheep derived from the original Spanish stock. Known for their ability to live and adapt in extreme climates, these sheep can be shorn twice a year instead of once. They are very personable animals and make good mothers. Many ewes produce twins and triplets. Some rams have four horns, a rare trait among sheep breeds. Their distinctive, longhaired wool has a soft undercoat and a protective overcoat. Wool colors come in an amazing assortment, including white, beige, medium brown, brown, reddish brown, apricot, dark brown-black, white with black fibers, and silver. The wool is superior for its glossy fibers, strength, and

durability. It is low in lanolin, which cuts down on washing and time-consuming carding.

Navajo-Churro sheep are recognized as a breed by the American Sheep Industry. Thanks to the careful sheepherding and breeding practices of the *Diné* for more than 300 years, the Navajo-Churro sheep have evolved into the best wool providers for weavers in the world. **Black Mesa** (Big Mountain or *Dziłíjiin*), **Arizona**, gets its name from the coal veins running through the earth. **The Black Mesa Weavers** are traditional *Diné* who raise Churro sheep and sell their products—wool and weavings—around the world.

Clans – a kinship system. Traditionally, individuals who share a common clan do not date or marry. Navajos are said to be born to a certain clan (mother's clan) and born for a certain clan (father's clan). The mother's clan is the primary clan. Besides the primary clan, Navajo people with Navajo parents have three more clans—their father's clan, the clan of their mother's father, and the clan of their father's father.

Cradleboard – a baby carrier oftentimes made of cedar wood. The strip of wood arched over the top end of the cradleboard, known as the *rainbow*, protects the baby's head and face.

Dibé – sheep.

Diné – (Den-nay) Navajo word for *the People*.

Diné Bizaad – the native language of the Navajo.

***Diné* Colleges** – eight colleges located in the Navajo Nation. The main campus is in Tsaile, Arizona. The colleges recently expanded to offer limited, four-year degrees.

Dinéteh (also ***Diné Bikeyah***) – the land of the Navajo.

Family Organization – the Navajo family structure differs from the usual Western model and is strongly matriarchal. Cousins are called *cousin-brothers* and *cousin-sisters*. Grown sisters and brothers consider each other's children the same as their own children. The literal translation for the mother's sister (aunt) is *little Mother*. The mother's mother is referred to as *ma'sani'* (in several forms) or *old mother*, while the father's parents are the *nallys*.

Female Rain – a gentle, easy rain.

Hagoonee – good-bye.

Hózhó – Peace and harmony.

Hogan – a Navajo structure used as a home or for ceremonies. It may be made of logs, planks, metal, plywood, mud, or siding. **Note:** Because Navajo people have a disdain of death and a respect for the dead, they may traditionally abandon their home (hogan) if a person dies inside. In that case, no part is re-used. The door is boarded shut, and the smoke hole is plugged to keep the dead person's *chindi* trapped inside. The corpse is removed through a hole in the north wall called the *corpse hole*.

Kéét'éego – passing on knowledge; allowing people to learn from watching.

Klizzie – goat.

Lichen – (LIE-kin) combines two life forms: fungi and algae. It can grow anywhere, but it is usually found on rocks and trees. Colors range from red, bright orange or yellow, to dull gray or green. It is one of the natural ingredients collected by the Navajos to make dye.

Loco – a common slang word for crazy.

Locoweed – a wild herb taking its name from the Spanish word, loco, meaning crazy. Genus: Oxytropis, growing mostly in the Rocky Mountains and parts of the Great Plains. The neurotoxin (swainsonine) in locoweed causes unpredictable behavior, violence, and other symptoms. Most ranchers destroy locoweed to protect their animals.

Lupine – a plant growing in elevations above 4,000 feet. It has a distinctive flower and grows in five-foot tall bushy plants or in miniature versions close to the ground. Used in making dyes.

Malachite – a green-colored, crystallized mineral.

Mesa – Spanish word for *table*. A mesa is a hill or small mountain with a flat, tabletop shape.

Mordant – a substance that helps seal in dye colors. Some are made from boiled juniper twigs or water and alum.

Mosí – (moe-see) cat.

Nalí – (nahl-lee) a name for a paternal grandmother.

Navajo Nation – the Navajo Nation (*Diné Bikeyah*) is about the size of West Virginia and the largest reservation in the United States. It is comprised of 16.2 million acres, occupies parts of thirteen counties, and is located in three states: Arizona, New Mexico, and Utah—with the largest area in Arizona. It is 27,000 square miles of desert and mountain, spectacular views, lakes, canyons, and mesas. It encompasses many renewable and non-renewable natural resources, including coal, oil, and natural gas. Much of the Navajo Nation is still extremely isolated, though it continues to make impressive educational and technical strides forward.

Outfit – when used in western vernacular, *outfit* refers to a family dwelling, often a ranch or farm. On the Rez, one's *outfit* may consist of a combination of one or more of the following structure(s): house, hogan, barn, shed, trailer, sheep pen, corral, and cattle chutes.

Petroglyphs – rock carvings or line drawings made by ancient people.

Pinion Nuts – (pin-yoehn) nuts shaken from pinion pine trees and gathered in the fall. A high-protein, long-standing food of the Southwest. Usually roasted. Pinion pine trees have distinctive pine needles.

Powwow – a social gathering featuring competitive dancing, foods and celebration. A powwow reflects the talent and culture of Native Americans.

Rabbitbrush (also, **chamisa**) – an erect, densely branched deciduous shrub with small clustered yellow heads and grey, velvety leaves. Mature flowers are boiled for at least six hours to produce a lemon-yellow dye. Immature buds or twigs give the dye a greenish tinge.

Rez – Slang for *Reservation*.

Rice Grass – a wild grass that has served as a food source since Anasazi times. Seeds are big enough to eat in May. The grass resembles a tangle of thread.

Saltbush – (fourwing saltbush) a perennial shrub with many medicinal uses and edible seeds with four "wings" coming out of the seed head. The leaves of the saltbush have a salty taste. It is a popular food source for deer, antelope, and rabbits. It provides shelter for many varieties of birds and small animals. Very hardy, the shrubs grow to various heights and can have a five- to six-foot spread. Weavers make shades of yellow dyes by boiling the leaves and flowers with alum.

Sheep Shears – a made-up expression used by Silki and Birdie.

Sheep's Wool – Auntie Jane's favorite made-up expression.

Shimasani – one of many familiar Navajo words for a maternal grandmother.

Slot Canyon – a narrow canyon formed over time by water (rain or flash floods) slowly cutting through rock. Though beautiful, these canyons are extremely dangerous during rainy season.

Sugar Rocks – (slang) a certain kind of rock, possibly gallent, or sandstone, that sparkles from crystallized particles inside.

Sumac – a tall bush found in shady canyons and alcoves. Highly useful, its red berries are eaten with sugar or cooked with cornmeal. Baskets are woven from the branches; yellow dye can be made from the roots; black dye from the twigs, leaves, and berries.

Two Grey Hills Rugs – Two Grey Hills (or Greyhills) rugs are woven in the Two Grey Hills area of the Navajo Nation. The **Two Grey Hills weavers** are famous for spinning the tightest yarns and for creating beautiful designs. Their all-natural wool colors are the same as their local sheep: shades of tan, grey, brown, black, and white. A Two Grey Hills rug tends to stand out considerably from other regional styles because the wool used for the yarn is finely carded and spun.

U.S.M.C. – United States Marine Corps.

Wol-la-chee – Navajo word for *ant*; Silki and Birdie's secret code name for the Ancient Ant Man.

Ya'at'eeh – (*yah-tay*; *tay* rhymes with *day*; sometimes *yah-uh-tay*) hello or hey; a goodwill greeting.

   *Note: *Ya'at'eeh* is not pronounced as "yah-tuh-hay." That pronunciation is known in *Dinéteh* as *the John Wayne pronunciation*.

About the Author

Personal

My love affair with the Arizona high country and its people began early. I had the good fortune to grow up in Apache County on a 50,000-acre cattle ranch wedged between the mysteriously gorgeous Navajo Nation and the stunning beauty of the White Mountain Apache Tribe Reservation, home of the rare Apache Trout. My friends were Native American and Hispanic, with a few Anglos thrown in for good measure.

When not riding horses, I often rode in the back of a pickup truck. Sometimes, we drove over terracotta roads so washed out they were barely drivable. You had to hold on for dear life or wind up on the ground. Those crazy bumps in the road were as fun as Disneyland to us.

A special place on the ranch was the White Rocks, the boulders I had in mind when I created Red Rocks for my protagonist, Silki. The White Rocks were magical—with tunnels, crawl spaces, petroglyphs, and a few blackened walls from ancient Anasazi fires. I gleaned tiny beads and arrowheads from sprawling anthills nearby, never tiring of watching the coppery colored ants toil to bring wondrous things back to their mounds.

My mother, Vivian, could rustle up enough food to feed a whole army of cowboys or any amount of visitors who showed up, strangely enough, just at suppertime. She was the finest cook in the whole region, but I thought in the whole world. Just a few of the foods we ate back then were pinto beans, sourdough bread dripping with fresh cow butter, range-raised beef, home-raised chicken (and dumplings), venison, Indian fry bread, and Concho chilies and peppers so hot you sweated under your lower eyelashes when you ate them. Our corn, squash, lettuce, green onions, carrots and every other vegetable you could think of grew out of red sand watered by the best-tasting well water around.

Looking back, our rural ranching community up on the Mogollon Rim near the White Mountains region was like another world. Our nearest town of Concho, Arizona, had a trading post that also functioned as a gas station, US post office, and candy counter for all the kids. Best things under creation were the solid cube cinnamon suckers sold from that counter. Concho had one school for all eight lower grades, a Catholic church, more crumbling adobe brick dwellings than usable ones, and the occasional cafe—none of which lasted very long.

At our ranch, the electricity was DC current provided by an old battery-operated generator and a wind charger. That meant no television, and rarely any radio. If we picked up any radio station at all, it was KOMA out of Oklahoma City at night. We had party-line telephones, so everyone knew everyone else's business. That kept all of us mucho friendly, I suppose.

Is it any wonder that I spent my childhood a little wild—and definitely crazy—galloping the winds of my imagination? Burnt sand, turquoise skies, and the delicious balm of cedar and juniper live in my heart and mind forever.

Professional

Before I settled into full-time novel writing, I traveled down many trails to satisfy my lifelong case of Terrible Curiosity. Those paths led me to court reporting, the Los Angeles garment industry, electro-mechanical drafting, journalism, homemaking, parenting two offspring, writing record album covers, western regional magazine writing, college humor-column writing (can't help it—I like making professors laugh) and the position of managing editor of a Fortune 500 corporate newsletter. Along the way, I picked up a Bachelor of Science degree in Business Management and graduated from the Institute of Children's Literature fiction writing curriculum. The Society of Children's Book Writers and Illustrators (SCBWI) and Women Writing the West (WWW) are my two special affiliations.